Lost—and Found

I rooted around in my backpack and pulled out a pair of binoculars. I used them to take a better look at the vehicle.

"It's a Seussmobile," I told Frank.

"What does that mean?"

"You know, it looks like something out of a Dr. Seuss book." What else was it supposed to mean?

Frank took the binoculars and checked out the van for himself. "See?" I asked. "It has all those weird metal things poking out all over it."

"I think they're solar panels," he said. "Which explains why we aren't hearing any motor."

It hadn't even registered with me how quiet the van was—but my brother was right. It was as silent as a submarine under water.

"There's a good chance we've found Arthur Stench," Frank told me. "Or he's about to find us."

THE *HARDY BOYS*
UNDERCOVER BROTHERS™

#1 *Extreme Danger*
#2 *Running on Fumes*

Available from Simon & Schuster

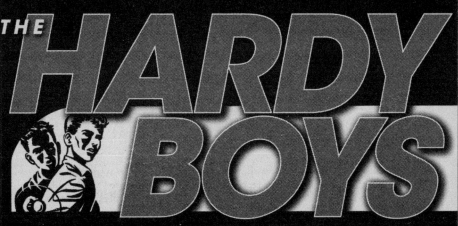

THE HARDY BOYS

UNDERCOVER BROTHERS™

#2   **Running on Fumes**

FRANKLIN W. DIXON

Aladdin Paperbacks
New York   London   Toronto   Sydney

This book is a work of fiction. Any references to historical events, real people, or real locales are used fictitiously. Other names, characters, places, and incidents are the product of the author's imagination, and any resemblance to actual events or locales or persons, living or dead, is entirely coincidental.

❧ALADDIN PAPERBACKS
An imprint of Simon & Schuster
Children's Publishing Division
1230 Avenue of the Americas
New York, NY 10020

THE HARDY BOYS MYSTERY STORIES and HARDY BOYS UNDERCOVER BROTHERS are trademarks of Simon & Schuster, Inc.
ALADDIN PAPERBACKS and colophon are trademarks of Simon & Schuster, Inc.
Designed by Lisa Vega
The text of this book was set in Aldine 401BT.
Manufactured in the United States of America
First Aladdin Paperbacks edition June 2005
10 9 8 7 6
Library of Congress Control Number: 2004113932
ISBN-13: 978-1-4169-0003-0
ISBN-10: 1-4169-0003-9

TABLE OF CONTENTS

Running on Fumes

1.

Crash or Burn

I grabbed the closest chair and hurled it at the huge window behind the desk.

Nothing. Not even a crack.

"Safety glass," I told my brother, Frank.

"Standard in an office building. Especially on the twenty-second floor," Frank answered. He didn't look up from the computer. His fingers scurried over the keyboard.

I grabbed the chair and slammed it against the glass again. *Bam! Bam! Bam!* I could feel the impact all the way up my arm bones to my shoulders.

The smell of smoke was getting stronger. We had to get out of here. The floor was shut down. The elevators were off—not that you should use elevators in a fire. The doors to the stairs were locked tight.

Somebody wanted us dead.

"Break, you piece of rat poop! Break!" I swung the chair like it was a bat and I was trying to knock the ball out of the stadium.

Yeah! Finally, a hairline fracture appeared in the glass. I beat on the place where the glass had weakened. The crunch of the glass under the chair was the best sound I'd ever heard.

"Frank—we've got an escape hatch."

I stuck my head through the shattered window and my stomach shriveled into the size of a BB. It was probably a tenth of a mile to the ground. And take it from me—when it's a tenth of a mile straight down, it's a long, long way.

"You've got the chutes, right?" I asked Frank.

He grunted. He doesn't appreciate my sense of humor. Maybe 'cause he has none himself!

"Okay, so . . . rope. We need rope," I muttered.

We were going to need rope if we were going to rappel down the side of the building.

Problem is, your average high-powered—and totally corrupt—lawyer's office doesn't come with rope. I scanned the room looking for a substitute. Cords off the two standing lamps, maybe? I snatched the letter opener off the massive wooden desk and started hacking away at the closest cord. Smoke was starting to creep into the room from under the door. Not much time left. Why couldn't the office have steel doors like the stairwells did?

"How's it going, Frank?" I asked as I started to work on the second electrical cord.

"This firewall is like nothing I've ever seen before. Elegant," my brother answered, eyes still glued to the monitor.

"I'm more worried about the firewall on the other side of the door!" I shot back.

"I gotta get through it." The keys clacked under Frank's fingers. "If I don't—"

He didn't finish the sentence. But I knew what would happen if he didn't get through that firewall to the list of witnesses.

You worry about getting you and Frank out of here alive, I ordered myself. *Let him worry about the witnesses.*

With a figure-eight knot I tied the two pieces of cord together. The combined length would get us down about a story and a half. That left nineteen and a half stories to go.

Wait. Twenty and a half. I'd forgotten about the lobby.

I yanked the cord out of the phone. The phone was dead anyway. Another piece of the kill-Frank-and-Joe-Hardy plan. I guess it wouldn't have done much good to trap us in a burning building if we could just call the fire department.

I strode around the room, jerking the cord free from the little metal staples that held it to the wall. *That'll get me another few stories,* I thought as I added the phone cord to my rope.

The computer had some decent cordage I could use. But I couldn't have it until Frank was done. And even with that, we still needed more.

What else? What else?

The carpet that covered a big section of the polished wood floor. Perfect! But it would take me hours to cut it into strips with a letter opener. . . .

Wait—I'd just busted through a window. There were shards of glass everywhere! I snagged a piece and set to work on the carpet. Good thing it was thin.

You'd think hitting the ground would save me from the smoke—but there was no escape. In seconds my eyes were watering. Each breath was like swallowing sandpaper.

I ripped off my shirt and hoisted myself onto my feet. I'd spotted a mini-fridge in here the first time I'd visited Frank on his intern job. That was his cover—high school intern at the law firm. Mine was annoying brother of high school intern.

I dashed to the fridge and helped myself to two bottles of water.

"Frank! Heads up!" I tossed him one of the bottles and poured one on my shirt. I used the shirtsleeves to tie the damp cloth over my face and then got back to work.

I tied the strips of carpet together as fast as I could. Added them to the rope.

Still not enough.

I added strips of the heavy drapes. The smoke was as thick as fog now. Orange-tinted fog. The flames were eating the door to the office. Any second they'd start on the ceiling.

"I'm through!" Frank called, voice muffled by the wet shirt tied over his mouth and nose. "Just got to copy the names." He hit a few keys, and the file started to download onto a CD.

I tied one end of my rope to one leg of the desk. "Nothing to use as a hook in here, right?" It's not like I could make some strong metal rings out of paper clips. "We'll have to Dulfersitz."

"File's done," the computer announced.

A second later Frank had the CD in his hand. I added all the computer cables to my rope. I still wasn't sure it was long enough to get us to the ground.

"Go, go, go!" Frank ordered.

I didn't have to be told twice. I wrapped the rope around my body and under my butt; the *sitz* part of the Dulfersitz rappelling technique means you sit on the rope.

Then I took a deep breath, turned around, and climbed out the window.

The breeze was strong up there, swinging me out to the left. I managed to get my feet positioned against the building and started to slide down the rope. Moving from phone cord to carpet to curtain to computer cord to . . .

To nothing.

No more rope. And my feet hadn't hit the pavement yet. I twisted my head around, trying to see the ground.

"Joe! Jump!" Frank shouted.

I looked up and saw that the cloth part of the rope had started to burn above my brother's hands. Frank needed me out of his way. Stat.

I closed my eyes and let go.

2.

Fatal Blow

"Good morning, morning glory. Time to get up."

I rolled over and checked my alarm clock. "I have three more minutes," I called to Aunt Trudy. And I wanted every second of them.

Aunt Trudy pushed open the door. "I am not letting you be late when you have finals, Frank. And that's that."

I knew the progression. If I didn't get up now, Aunt Trudy would pull off the covers. If I still didn't get up, she'd dump a glass of water over my head.

"Okay, I'm up. I'm up." I sprang to my feet. Other than extreme lack of sleep and a smoke-fried throat, I felt pretty good.

7

Aunt Trudy nodded her approval. "No backsie-insies," she warned as she left my room. Sometimes Aunt Trudy thinks I'm still five years old. Although I have to admit, it was sort of tempting to crawl back into the sheets.

Instead I pulled on my jeans and a clean shirt, then trotted down the hall. I couldn't stop myself from cracking up when I spotted Joe halfway down the stairs. His blond hair was plastered to his head with water. Aunt Trudy got him good.

Plus, he was limping.

"Hey, are you all right?" I asked as I caught up to him. "As all right as possible after crash-landing onto a cement sidewalk and then having you crash-land on top of me," Joe answered.

He was careful to keep his voice low. Aunt Trudy and our mom don't know anything about the missions Joe and I take on for ATAC. They've never even heard of the American Teens Against Crime organization. Even though Dad is the one who founded it.

ATAC is top secret. The whole reason the squad exists is because teenagers can get into certain places adults can't, no questions asked. If everybody knew there were teen crime fighters around, that wouldn't be true anymore.

We grabbed our backpacks on the way out the

front door and almost tripped over Mom. She had the whole veranda covered with junk.

Well, I call it junk. Mom thinks of it as treasure.

"Careful," Mom said. "I just got the aluminum and the tin divided." She pointed to two of the piles of trash.

"You don't have to separate those, do you?" Joe asked. "Metal is metal to the recycling plant."

"Yes, but the kids are going to make luminarias out of the tin cans at the library's after-school program," Mom explained.

"Recycling isn't just throwing things into the blue garbage can," she continued. I'm saving up corks from wine bottles to make a bulletin board." Mom nodded toward another one of her piles. "And I'm thinking of making picture frames out of those CD cases."

"Merry Christmas!" Playback, our parrot, called from his perch in the sun. "Ho, ho, ho!"

"It's June," I told the bird. He ignored me.

"And don't give her any ideas," Joe added, smiling at Playback.

"Ho, ho, ho!" Playback said again. He sounded freakishly like Aunt Trudy. She'd spent the holidays ho-ho-ho-ing. The parrot can imitate anything. You should hear his impression of the doorbell.

"Okay, no CD-case picture frames for Joe next Christmas," Mom said. "How do you feel about a wastepaper basket made of egg cartons?"

Joe groaned. Mom laughed.

"Come on," I told my brother. We carefully began weaving our way around the piles and headed toward the front steps.

A squawk cut through the air—and it didn't come from Playback.

Aunt Trudy rushed across the porch, knocking the tin cans into the tower of used foil.

"I can't believe I let you two sleep so late that you don't have time for breakfast. And on the day of your finals!" Aunt Trudy shoved sports bottles into our hands. "At least drink some water. You can't think clearly when you're dehydrated. I told your father that this morning. But would he listen? No!"

"Where is Dad, anyway?" Joe asked.

I took a swig of water so Aunt Trudy would calm down.

"One of his breakfasts with the other retired cops," Mom said. She started to get her piles back in order.

"Breakfast." Aunt Trudy snorted. "Donuts and black coffee in some diner with sticky tables. As if that counts as a decent breakfast!"

I doubted he was there, though. Dad usually said he was meeting up with friends from the force when he had ATAC business himself. I knew he'd be disappointed that he didn't get to hear the details of Joe's and my mission first thing.

"Drink! Drink!" Aunt Trudy urged.

I took another long swallow, tasting smoke along the way. I wondered how long that would last.

"Your Aunt Trudy is right," Mom agreed. "The body needs water for transporting hormones, chemical messengers, and nutrients. Did you know the brain is eighty-five percent water?"

Can you tell our mom is a research librarian?

"With prolonged dehydration, the brain cells actually start to shrink," she told us.

I drained the rest of the bottle, and I heard Joe slurping down his.

"Thanks, Aunt T," Joe said. It came out sounding like Auntie. "Now my brain cells are nice and fat and ready to kick it on those finals!"

Aunt Trudy beamed.

"See you later," I called over my shoulder.

"Wimps! Wimps! Wimps!" Playback called in farewell. Must have been something he picked up from his previous owner. Nothing to do with me and Joe.

I mean, do you know any wimps who ride

11

motorcycles? Motorcycles with hydraulic clutch. Optimized suspension. Fog lamps with flint protectors. Hazard warning. Digital CD player and CB radio.

Didn't think so!

Joe and I climbed on our bikes and roared off to school. Well, roared off at the speed limit. Teenage guys riding motorcycles are traffic cop bait. Just FYI.

"I'm not liking how that looks," Joe said when we parked our bikes in the school lot.

I followed his gaze. I didn't like the scene either. Brian Conrad was talking to our friend Chet Morton.

The thing is, guys like Brian never talk to guys like Chet. Guys like Brian insult guys like Chet. They bully guys like Chet. They punch guys like Chet.

But talk? No.

I hurried over to them. Joe was right behind me.

"I think I saw you looking at my sister," we arrived in time to hear Brian say. He was right in Chet's face. Chet's pale face.

Chet's a great guy and everything. But he hasn't ever figured out that the way to deal with the Brians in the world is to show no fear.

"Belinda isn't Chet's type," Joe jumped in.

Brian whipped his head toward Joe. "You're saying my sister isn't good enough for this dillweed?"

Chet took the opportunity to move away from Brian—and closer to Joe and me.

"Everyone knows Belinda is gaga over my brother here."

I felt heat flood up my neck. *Don't let me be blushing.* That's all I could think. *Do not let me be blushing.*

I have this thing. This minor problem. I kind of turn into a moron around girls. Especially hot girls like Belinda. Even hearing Joe talk about her and me . . . Well, you can't get more moronic than blushing.

"I don't get it myself. Everyone knows I'm the better-looking one," Joe added.

The bell rang.

"I don't want any of the three of you sniffing around Belinda." Brian nailed each of us with a look that was supposed to be chilling. He kept his eyes on me the longest.

Like I'd even attempt to talk to Belinda. Not because I was scared of Brian, but because I was scared of making a total fool out of myself.

I held Brian's stare until he turned and walked away.

"So *were* you checking out Belinda?" Joe asked Chet as we headed inside.

"Hey, she was checking *me* out. I was just standing there." Chet flexed—as if he had muscles to flex.

Yeah, right, I thought. Chet's a good friend, but he's kind of a dork sometimes.

I mean, he was all attitude now that he was alone with me and Joe. But I noticed he couldn't stop himself from looking over his shoulder. To make sure Brian hadn't heard.

"See you guys at lunch," I said when we reached the door to my first-period class.

Chemistry. Final number one.

It wasn't that hard. At least not with my super-hydrated brain. Which was lucky, because Joe and I hadn't gotten much studying done last night.

Make that no studying. None. Although the story for Mom and Aunt Trudy was that we'd come home so late because we'd pulled a late-night study fest at Chet's.

English was a little more difficult. But only because I sit behind Belinda in English. And that's sort of distracting.

Next up, PE. A break from the brainwork. Nice. I was looking forward to it. That is, until I found out we were fencing. And who did Mr. Zwick assign to be my fencing partner?

Yep. Brian Conrad.

I slid my mesh-front mask into place. Brian and I faced off.

"Don't forget what I said this morning, Hardy." Brian thrust his foil at me. Going on the attack.

I parried. Now it was my turn to attack.

"Have you ever noticed how people who talk all the time never actually do anything?" I asked.

I jabbed my foil and hit Brian on the arm. That didn't count. To get a point in fencing, you have to touch the tip of your foil to the torso of your opponent. Head and arms don't get you any points.

"If my sister could see you now, she'd get over her little crush. She goes for jocks."

I didn't bother to reply.

Brian came at me again. I blocked. Thrust. He blocked.

We circled each other, foils clashing. A line of sweat trickled down my back as the clanging of metal on metal filled my ears. Brian's eyes stayed on mine. I could see them through the double layers of mesh—mine and his.

Then he glanced left. I jerked my foil in that direction, sure he was going to strike that way.

Instead he brought the foil to my heart. "If this was a real fight, you'd be dead," Brian announced. "This steel would slice right through your heart." He turned and walked away.

I was still thinking about his words at lunch when I met up with Joe at my locker. *If this was a real fight, you'd be dead.*

Brian was right. If there hadn't been protective tips on our foils . . . if I hadn't been wearing padding . . . if we hadn't been just two guys in gym class . . .

I would be dead right now. I'd blown it.

I twirled in the combination and opened my locker. Brian's voice continued in my head. *This steel would slice right through your heart.*

My heart.

I blinked twice. It was still there.

There was a heart inside my locker.

3.

THE NEXT ASSIGNMENT

"Oooh! Frank's got a secret admirer."

I reached for the big, red, heart-shaped box of candy jammed in the bottom of my brother's locker. "I call the ones with nuts."

Frank slapped my hand away.

"Is there a note?" I asked. "A mushy note? 'Oh, how I love you, Frankie, baby, honey, dollface.' Whoever sent it is calendar-challenged. Valentine's Day isn't this week."

Frank blushed. My brother actually blushes.

And girls still like him. I seriously don't get it.

He opened the heart-shaped box. And suddenly I wasn't thinking about girl psychology anymore.

There was no candy in the box. Only a nice wad of cash, a folded map, and a video game disc. The label on the front read: RUNNING ON FUMES.

We were about to get our next ATAC assignment. This is how they always came. Disguised as video games.

"We need some privacy." Frank led the way out onto the quad and over to the oak tree at the far corner.

I pulled my portable game player out of my backpack and plopped down on the grass. Frank sat next to me and handed over the "game." I slid it into the slot.

I love the sound of that click when the disc is in place. My heart actually starts to beat faster. Every single time. I never get tired of the moment when we're about to find out the next assignment.

I hit PLAY. The Earth appeared on the small screen. A small blue and white ball. Spinning.

That didn't tell me much. Our assignment was somewhere in the world. Duh.

"Humans share the earth with as many as one hundred million other species." As the narrator spoke, trees and fungus and animals and insects and single-cell organisms took over the screen, new ones appearing every second. Filling every inch.

"But two hundred and seventy thousand of these species become extinct every year." Red Xs slashed across the monitor, crossing out creatures I hadn't even known existed in the first place.

"This extreme extinction rate has occurred only five times before in the history of the earth, caused by meteors, volcanic eruptions, or rapid climate change."

"Meteors. That's one of the theories about what killed off the dinosaurs," Frank commented.

"Thanks, Mom." Sometimes my brother sounds like a research librarian himself. "What I want to know is what this has to do with us."

"But nature has nothing to do with the massive extinction going on today," the narrator continued. I couldn't get my eyes off all those red Xs. How could that many species disappear every year?

Entire *species*. It made my head hurt to think about it.

"The current extinction explosion is caused by"— a photo of Frank and me appeared—"humans."

"Somebody at the home office has a warped sense of humor," Frank said.

"I'm still not seeing the connection to us," I complained. "What's the mission?"

Pictures of tons more people appeared on the screen. "Humans consume nearly half of all the Earth's resources. This man wants to change all that. His name is Arthur Stench."

One man replaced all the people filling the screen. He looked like he was in his fifties. He was losing his hair, but he had a long beard—with enough hair for his whole body. It looked like he worked out.

"Arthur Stench has a compound in the California desert. It's a place where people gather to live in harmony with the land. Where they can give back to the earth."

I felt like giving the game player a shake. Was I watching a PBS special or what? Where was the assignment?

Stench's photo faded and a picture of a desert came up. All scrubby brush and cactus and rocks, with some mountains in the background.

"We have no visual of the actual compound. Visitors are not welcome. That's where you two come in. Many of Stench's followers are teenagers. Your assignment is to infiltrate the compound."

"I don't get it," I said. "Stench sounds like one of the good guys."

It was like the narrator had heard me. "Stench may be a harmless man. Even a hero. But we have received information about his using extreme measures to force people into following his beliefs. Threats. Arson. Bombing. Even murder. We need to put an end to it. But first, we need to determine whether or not he really is a threat."

"So it's not all about recycling," I muttered. I stared at Stench's picture, like if I stared at it long enough, I'd be able to see into his brain.

"There are no roads leading to the compound. You won't find any hotels or fast-food places. It's

SUSPECT PROFILE

<u>Name:</u> Arthur Stench

<u>Hometown:</u> Santa Cruz, California

<u>Physical description:</u> Caucasian, age 55, 5'9", 175 lbs., balding, beard, left-handed, muscular.

<u>Occupation:</u> Leader of the Heaven compound.

<u>Background:</u> Both parents died while he was attending the University of Southern California; founded several companies that went bankrupt; divorced; estranged from children; antitechnology.

<u>Suspicious behavior:</u> House has no windows; needs a bodyguard so must have enemies; overheard making threats against oil companies.

<u>Suspected of:</u> Ecoterrorism.

<u>Possible motives:</u> Willing to use violence to enforce his beliefs if that is what it takes.

unlikely you'll see any people until you arrive. We recommend using your motorcycles."

Our juiced-up bikes appeared on the screen, flying across the desert. No roads—no speed limits! Cool.

"This mission, like every mission, is top secret. In five seconds this disc will be reformatted into a regular music CD."

Exactly five seconds later, some Cher song started playing at top volume.

I heard a few laughs from some of the other kids on the quad before I could rip the disc out of the player.

"You know what this means?" Frank's dark brown eyes were gleaming.

"Yes, I do, my friend. It means—"

"Road trip!" we said together.

No boring stay-at-home summer for us. We were taking the bikes all the way across the country. How excellent was that?

4.

Good or Evil?

Joe flopped down on my bed the next morning. Without bothering to take his shoes off. Did I mention my brother is a slob?

"Got the GPS on both bikes programmed," he announced. He blew a big purple bubblegum bubble. The hypercharged fake grape smell almost made me sneeze.

He sucked the gum back into his mouth and started chomping. "The route is 2,741.3 miles. Almost a two-day drive."

"If you drive nonstop. Without eating. Or sleeping," I corrected him. I slid a set of lock-picking tools into my backpack. They'd been useful on other missions, and I liked having them along.

"I was thinking about that. I know we need to

get out to the compound and check things out. But we probably have a little time to—"

"—see some stuff," I finished for him. I was totally with Joe on this one. "I was thinking a little detour to Mount Rushmore might be nice."

"Wait." Joe used the corner of my bedspread to clean out one of his ears. "Say that again."

"You're washing that." Joe kept on cleaning, but I didn't bother repeating myself. I knew he'd heard me just fine.

"We have the whole country to see. And a bunch of stone heads are at the top of your list? Unbelievable."

I added some underwear to my pack. Joe was probably planning on wearing the same pair of boxers for the whole ten days. He thought if you turned them inside out it made them clean again.

"What's at the top of your list?" I asked him.

Joe sat up. "Okay, tell me if this is not cool. I read about this place where they train animals for fairs and stuff. All the tic-tac-toe-playing chickens come from there."

"You'd rather see farm animals playing the dumbest game imaginable than go to one of the most famous places in the country?"

Before he could answer, Mom came into the room. "I printed out some info on petroglyphs for you guys. Some of them could have been carved eight thousand years ago."

I felt my face getting hot. It's not just being around girls that makes me blush. Lying to Mom does it too.

Joe and I had told her we wanted to use part of our summer break to check out the petroglyphs in the Mojave Desert. The designs Native Americans had chipped into rocks sounded pretty cool.

But that's not why we had chosen this cover story. We picked it for two reasons. One: Mom was likely to approve something so educational. And two: There were petroglyphs in the same general area as the compound.

If you're gonna lie, it's better to put some truth in there.

Joe took the printouts from Mom and started scanning them. "Is any of this talk about the connection between the petroglyphs and aliens true? I heard that some of the glyphs are actually of UFOs the Indians had seen."

Can you tell my brother is a fan of Art Bell? That guy's talk show is all about UFOS and conspiracies and how there are real vampires roaming around. Joe eats that stuff up with a big spoon.

"Actually, I did come across one site that talked about 'glyphs and aliens," Mom told Joe. "I didn't print anything, but there's some great stuff about how some archeologists think the petroglyphs were drawn by medicine men while they were in a trance state."

"You mean they were wasted?"

"Well, there may have been some mind-altering plants used in some of the ceremonies," Mom admitted.

I zipped my backpack and slung it over one shoulder. "Ready?" I asked Joe.

"Yep." He grabbed his own backpack off the floor and stuffed Mom's printouts in the front pocket.

"I guess I don't have to give you any mother speeches. Like, always wear your helmets. And try to eat something that's not fried once in a while."

"Don't worry. Aunt Trudy's made her mark on us," I told her.

"You know when you two are gone it's *me* she lectures," Mom complained.

"She means well," Joe teased. That's what Mom always tells us when we complain about Aunt Trudy. We love our aunt and everything, but she can be a pain sometimes.

I was surprised Aunt Trudy wasn't upstairs right at that moment, supervising the packing. Her absence was explained when we headed outside.

She was already out there, polishing the handlebars of Joe's motorcycle.

It took us fifteen minutes to get through all the good-byes and Aunt Trudy lectures and Mom suggestions. It would have taken longer if Dad hadn't been at another one of his "breakfasts." He always has a lot of advice before a mission.

We were outta there.

Once I'm on my bike, I never want to get off. It's nothing like riding in a car. It's like the motorcycle is an extension of your own body. Like you're running down the highway. Wind blasting past you. We'd been riding for a day and a half now—with a short stop for sleep—and I still wasn't tired of the bike. I could ride forever.

Our first major stop was Mount Rushmore. Joe and I had made a deal—we got to alternate destinations on the way across the country.

And, yeah, he was right. Mount Rushmore was just a bunch of big stone heads.

But big stone heads of men who helped make America what it is. Washington. Lincoln. Jefferson. Theodore Roosevelt. It was like being in the presence of a hundred and fifty years of history.

"Okay, my turn now," Joe said when we got on our bikes in the monument's parking lot.

"The brainiac chickens, right?"

"Nope. Even better. The Thing in the Desert."

"I need more information."

"It's this *thing*. Someone found it in the desert. It's supposed to be amazing."

"But what is it?"

"That's what's so cool." Joe pulled on his helmet. "It's indescribable. You have to see it for yourself. People come from all over."

"Where did you even hear about it?"

Joe tapped his helmet. He couldn't hear me.

Whatever. It was his pick.

When we hit Arizona, we started seeing signs for the Thing. YOU ARE A HUNDRED MILES AWAY FROM THE THING IN THE DESERT. WHAT IS THE MYSTERY OF THE DESERT? That kind of stuff. None of the billboards gave any indication of what this famous thing actually was.

About twenty-two billboards later, we finally arrived at a big gas-station–souvenir-shop combo. Joe was practically dancing as we headed inside. We each paid two bucks and started following the big green footprints that we were told would take us to the Thing.

"How cool is this?" Joe asked, making sure to place his feet right inside the monster tracks.

"Right now all I'm seeing is pieces of wood that are supposed to look like animals." I squinted at the closest log. I guess it looked sort of like a squirrel. A mutant squirrel.

"You're the one who wanted to see rocks that looked like heads." Joe picked up his pace. The monster tracks led us out of the shed we were in and into another one. We passed some bedroom furniture from France. And a car that Hitler supposedly rode in once. Maybe.

Finally, in shed number three, we reached the Thing. I'm sure you all want to know what exactly it is, right?

Sorry. I can't tell you. I couldn't figure it out.

It's kind of a mummy. Maybe. With possibly a mummy baby. The sign above it says, YOU DECIDE.

Great.

I looked over at Joe, figuring he'd be ready to demand his money back. Or at least admit that Mount Rushmore was a much better destination.

"That thing is unholy *awesome*!" he declared.

Okay, so I was wrong. But at least the next destination pick was mine. Had to wait for the trip back, though. We needed to get our butts in gear and get to Arthur Stench's compound.

We decided to continue on to Phoenix, then crash. The next day we'd have about a four-and-a-half-hour ride to Palm Springs. Stench's group was set up in the desert, about another hour from the city.

"So, want to place a bet?" Joe asked when we stepped into our motel room.

"On what?" I pulled off my boots and stretched out on the closest bed. It felt like the mattress was vibrating. It always takes a while for the sensation of being on my bike to fade.

"On what we're going to find tomorrow." Joe did his usual shoes-on bed flop.

Didn't bother me this time. Wasn't my bed-spread.

"Do you think Stench will be just some tree-loving guy? All peaceful? Or do you think he'll have a tent full of bombs and stuff?"

"I don't think ATAC would have sent us out here if there wasn't some chance the guy is dirty," I answered. "Not that I'm complaining. It's been a great trip."

"I knew you were grooving on the Thing!"

"The gift shop was better. Too bad we didn't have enough cash for that stuffed rattler."

"Yeah," Joe agreed. "Although Aunt Trudy probably would have made us keep it in the garage."

I closed my eyes. The image of Arthur Stench filled the blackness behind my eyelids. Good guy? Bad guy?

Trying to protect the earth was definitely good. But not if you used violence to do it.

The image of Arthur Stench seemed to smile at me. Daring me to figure him out.

Tomorrow Joe and I would get the chance. We'd be face-to-face with Stench.

5.

BLOWOUT

I didn't have to look at the GPS to know we were getting close. Hundreds of white windmills stretched out over the desert.

This had to be the San Gorgonio Pass. Frank had been telling me about it last night. I was having trouble falling asleep. Adrenaline was pumping through me just thinking about what we might find at the compound.

When I'm feeling that way, one thing that can calm me down is hearing Frank yammer. He comes up with some interesting stuff sometimes. And last night he filled me in on the windmills.

I told you he's part reference librarian, right? The good thing is, he's part cop, too. A solid combo.

But anyway, before all the facts conked me out,

I got the scoop on the wind turbines. It's pretty amazing. See, hot air rises over the Coachella Valley and forces cooler air through a pass between the San Bernardino and San Jacinto mountains.

The wind gets up to twenty miles an hour. And that gets the windmills really spinning. The people who own the land sell the electricity the wind turbines generate. They farm wind.

I think next time my guidance counselor asks what career I have in mind, I'm going to say that. Wind farmer. But really, I'm pretty sure I'll end up a detective or a PI or something. I need the excitement.

Frank pulled up alongside me. He tapped his GPS. I looked down at mine.

Blank screen.

Uh oh.

I took the next exit off the highway and pulled into the first gas station I spotted. The first and only gas station. The exit hadn't even led to a town—just the station, and a diner that looked like it had been closed for fifty years. The newspaper over the windows was torn and yellow.

I checked the GPS again. Still dark. I was hoping the malfunction was a windmill thing. But no.

Frank rolled up behind me and took off his helmet. So did I. "Guess we're out of GPS signal range. We're going to have to do it the old-fashioned way," he said. He took the map that had been delivered with our assignment out of his backpack.

I leaned close so I could study it too. "Seems like we should get on this access road instead of the freeway."

"Yeah. Then we should see a road cutting into the desert a couple miles down." Frank returned the map to his backpack.

I started to put my helmet back on, then I hesitated. It seemed like we were dead center in the middle of nowhere. The dinky gas station was probably the last place to get supplies.

"I'm going to stock up on water," I told Frank.

"I'll fill up the bikes."

I headed into the little store—not much more than a couple of food racks and a fridge next to the cashier. The place smelled like unwashed feet.

I grabbed a few bottles of water and some sodas for each of us, along with an assortment of chips, some beef jerky, and some of those neon pink marshmallow cakes.

The old guy behind the counter rang up everything without comment. I paid for the grub and gas and returned to Frank. We stowed everything in our backpacks and headed for the access road.

It ran alongside the highway for a while. But unlike the highway, we had this road all to ourselves.

It was kind of cool—and kind of freaky. I mean, what kind of road has zero traffic?

Our bikes ate up the road, mile after mile.

Wait. Shouldn't we have made a turn by now? According to the map, we were supposed to go only a couple of miles before we hung a left.

Except there hadn't been any place to turn.

I slowed down a little. Frank brought his bike up even with mine. "Did you see a turn?" I shouted. He shook his head.

Maybe we'd underestimated the mileage. A paper map is no GPS. I checked the odometer. Watched as another mile clicked off. Then another.

Frank waved for me to pull over. "Whaddya think?" I asked when I came to a stop next to him.

"I think maybe one of those dirt tracks back there might actually have been a road."

"One of those things that looked like bunny trails?"

Frank had the map out again. "Has to be. At least if we believe the map."

I stared in frustration at the blank screen of the GPS. What good was the thing if it didn't work in isolated areas? Isolated areas were where you needed it most.

"So which bunny trail do we pick?" I asked Frank. "We went by about four of them."

He frowned. "I guess we do it by mileage. The road we're supposed to take is . . ." He laid his pinkie finger on the map, calculating. "I'd say it's three and a quarter miles back in the other direction."

We turned around. I watched the odometer click one, two, three miles. I scanned the left side of the access road. A fifth of a mile later I spotted a dirt path heading out into the desert.

It had to be what we were looking for. Clearly Frank thought so too. He swung his bike onto the trail.

I followed him, slowing down. The bumpy path wasn't made for speed. Good thing we were on our motorcycles. A car wouldn't have cut it.

I didn't really miss the speed, though—even though I usually want to go everywhere as fast as possible. I thought there wouldn't really be anything to look at in the desert, but I was wrong. There were those cacti that look like guys with their hands up. And these stunted spiky trees. Tumbleweeds. Actual tumbleweeds. Huge piles of boulders.

I was so busy looking around, it took me a minute to realize that Frank had come to a stop. I pulled my bike up next to his. Right away I saw what the problem was.

The road forked. On the map it didn't do that.

"You think we chose the wrong route?" I asked.

"This should be the right road. We calculated the mileage correctly."

I pulled out my cell phone. No juice.

"Well, the fork to the right heads more in the direction I think we're supposed to be going." I cracked open one of my sodas. The carbonation stung my dry throat.

"Yeah," Frank agreed. "We might as well try it. We can always turn around." He opened a bottle of water and drank. "Caffeine dehydrates you, you know. You should drink some water with that soda."

"Next stop." I drained the can, then took the lead down the trail we'd chosen. It got narrower. And narrower.

Then it disappeared.

Frank and I stopped for another strategy session. I took his advice and had some water and marsh-mallow cake.

We decided to go down the other path for a while before we returned to the access road. It was a good choice. The path headed in the wrong direction for about a mile and a half, but then it looped back.

I was pretty sure we were going the right way, but it would have been nice to see a road sign. There was nothing to indicate that any human had even been out here before.

The sun beat down on my helmet. I shrugged out of my leather jacket and used one hand to stow it in the container under my seat.

A long shadow appeared across the sand in front of me. At first I couldn't figure out what was casting it. Then I looked up.

A huge bird flew overhead. Black with an orange head and a wingspan that was wider than my whole body. Two of the bird's buddies joined it. *Vultures*, I realized.

I hoped they weren't after me and Frank.

A moment later I spotted exactly what the vultures were after. A sheep lay on the ground ahead of us. One of the vultures perched on its back. In an instant I could see a strip of the sheep's flesh in the bird's sharp beak.

I stopped for a closer look. How many times do you get to see vultures in action?

"That bighorn has to weigh more than two hundred pounds. Wonder what took it down," Frank said.

I eyed the sheep. Something other than vultures had already been eating it. "Isn't there a bear on the California state flag?" I asked.

"There are supposed to be some black bears out in the desert."

I looked over my shoulder. I felt like Chet, trying

to make sure Brian Conrad wasn't around.

The other two vultures swooped down on the sheep. There was a little squabbling with the first one about who got to eat what, then they settled down.

Probably whatever had killed the sheep wasn't around, or the vultures wouldn't be there. Right?

Maybe not. I heard a long, high, quavery howl. Followed up by a *yip, yip, yip.*

"Coyote," Frank said.

The vultures didn't seem too bothered by the sound.

"Four o'clock." My brother's voice was low and calm.

I turned my head to the right. A coyote was crouched beside some prickly-looking shrubs, its eyes on the sheep.

It gave another howl. The hair on my arms stood up, even though the coyote was only about the size of a collie. Same basic head and body shape too.

Now, don't go thinking I'm a wimp. But even though this coyote probably weighed in at about twenty pounds and looked kinda like a pet, I knew he had to be tough. Nobody was pouring him Alpo every night. He had to go out and hunt.

And he had the teeth to do it.

"It doesn't look interested in us. But we should probably—," Frank began.

"Yeah," I agreed. The coyote's yellow eyes shifted to me as I moved to start up the bike. He started toward me, belly low to the ground. In total stalking mode.

The hair on the back of my neck went up this time—and the hair on my arms hadn't even fallen back into place yet.

Stare back? Don't stare back? Yell? Don't yell?

Frank had chosen to be still and quiet, so I did too.

Looking directly into a dog's eyes is a dominance thing. I figured it was probably the same with a coyote, so I deliberately lowered my eyes.

Of course, I couldn't see if my strategy worked. The coyote could be about to leap on me. I shot a quick glance in the direction of the animal. I had to.

The coyote was moving toward the sheep. I let out a breath I didn't even know I was holding, then took the opportunity to rev up the bike. Frank and I left the birds and the coyote to duke it out over the sheep.

A few miles later we stopped again. I did a bear and coyote scan, then moved my eyes lower to check for rattlers and scorpions. All clear.

"Maybe we should go back and try another road," Frank said. "We should be heading southeast by now."

The sun was pretty much directly ahead of us. And since the sun still sets in the west, we had a problem.

I pulled out a couple of pieces of jerky and handed one to Frank. "What if we went off-road?" I asked. "Just headed in the right direction?"

Frank considered it. "I do have my compass. And we could make some markers with pieces of one of our shirts so we could find our way back."

"We're not using one of my shirts. You brought enough clean underwear to last you till the next millennium. We can use a few pairs of those."

I drank some water to wash down the Slim Jim. When I put the bottle back in my pack, I realized I'd just drunk half of the last one I had. I'd thought I had one more.

"What?" Frank asked.

"Just have to pace myself on the water," I answered.

"I have a bottle left."

"I have half of one and another soda. Plus three little bags of chips."

This would have been no biggie in normal circumstances. In normal circumstances there's at least a mini-mart within blocks. A mini-mart and a fast-food place.

But in the desert . . . there was nothing but desert.

I did another cell phone check. No juice. I knew that's what I'd see, but I had to look.

Frank pulled a pair of boxers out of his backpack. He used his Swiss Army knife to cut a strip of cloth. Then he tied the cloth to the closest cactus.

"We have enough hours of daylight to try your plan," he said. He climbed back on his bike.

We veered off the path and zoomed along. I felt like we could ride forever without hitting civilization.

Then I saw something that made me feel like cheering: a NO TRESPASSING sign nailed to a big cactus.

I let out a whoop and put on the brakes so hard that the bike skidded in a semicircle.

"You're happy that we have to turn around?" Frank asked.

"Don't you get it?" I asked. "That sign means that there's something to trespass onto! That means people. We can ask for directions. Get more water."

"You're right. Let's get trespassing!" Frank led the way past the sign.

A few miles later we saw another one: TURN BACK. PRIVATE PROPERTY. This sign was posted next to a road! It wasn't paved or anything, but it was a road.

I shot Frank a thumbs up. We were getting closer to . . . something.

I jammed on the gas. I could get a little speed going now. Yeah! I was flying down the flat, straight road.

Then—

Bang!

My back tire blew out.

I spun out of control.

6.

NO TRESPASSING

Suddenly I hit the dirt. The weight of my bike pinned me to the ground.

I killed the motor and looked over at Joe. He'd been tossed too.

"You okay?" I asked. I shoved the bike off and scrambled to my feet.

"Yeah." Joe sat on the ground next to his motorcycle. "What the heck just happened?"

I leaned over and examined my front tire. A small, sharp spike was imbedded in it. I jerked the spike free and held it up. "*This* just happened."

Joe found a similar spike in his back tire. "I guess when they said 'no trespassing,' they really meant it."

"No kidding." I walked back a few feet. Now

44

that I was looking for them, I saw a bunch of the spikes scattered in the dirt.

"So, do we walk deeper in, or back out?" Joe asked.

I thought about the one and a half bottles of water we had between us and the small amount of food. If you could call chips and candy food.

"In, I think. I'm hoping the guy who left these spikes is closer than the access road."

Joe nodded. "Yeah. It's not like the access road would even do us that much good. We didn't see anybody on it."

"We'd probably end up having to go back to that gas station."

And that was a lot of hiking. In the desert. With almost no water.

Stop thinking about the water, I ordered myself. It wasn't helping anything, but it kept slamming back into my brain.

No water basically equals death—no matter where you are. But in the desert, death comes faster.

We were on a mission, though. We couldn't turn back.

Joe picked up his bike, moved it to the side of the road, and hid it behind some brush. I moved mine, too. Don't get me wrong, it wasn't easy leaving them behind. We love our bikes. But we had business. And besides—who was around to steal them?

We started to walk.

And walk.

And walk.

Sweat dripped down my face and down my back. At least I was still sweating. You know your body is really going into crisis when you don't.

"What do you think? Drink the soda or not?" Joe asked.

"It'll just make you thirstier."

"I guess the chips are a bad idea."

"They'll definitely make you thirstier. But I guess we might need the carbs for energy."

"I'll save 'em," Joe decided.

Neither of us had mentioned the heat. What was the point in talking about it? But it was like a solid presence on top of my head. Pushing down. Making every step harder.

I got an idea. I pulled a T-shirt out of my backpack and wrapped it around my head. "You should do this too," I told Joe. "Use anything white. It will reflect the sun—keep you a little cooler."

He followed my lead, also using a T-shirt, and we kept walking.

And walking.

And walking.

I didn't like the way Joe was looking. He wasn't picking up his feet as he walked. Each step was stirring up the sand—which we both ended up breathing. His eyes seemed sort of sunken in, and his lips were cracked.

I probably looked about the same. I flashed on what Mom had said about water. How you need water to transport nutrients, and how your brain cells shrink without it.

How long did it take for that to happen? Joe and I needed to be sharp out here.

"Do you think ATAC would be able to find us out here?" Joe asked. "I mean, do you think we're ending up anywhere close to where we're supposed to be?"

"If the signs were put up by Stench and his group, we are," I answered. I didn't point out that ATAC—and Dad—weren't expecting us back for almost a week.

We kept on walking. That's all we could do.

Walking, walking, walking.

"Do you think ATAC would be able to find us?" Joe asked.

I shot a glance at him. Did he remember he'd already asked that question? Was he getting delirious?

I pulled my water bottle out of my backpack and

took a small swallow. Then I handed it to Joe. "You should drink a little."

"I still have some of mine."

"Go ahead. We'll share yours later."

Joe took a swig, then immediately coughed it back up. "Sorry," he muttered. "Wasted it."

"Try it again," I urged.

He managed to keep the next swallow down. When he handed back the bottle, I noticed that his skin felt clammy.

Not good.

I checked the compass. We were going southeast. But that didn't mean anything, because we didn't really know where we had started from. The map I kept looking at was useless.

I jabbed a piece of cloth onto one of the spines of the nearest cactus. If we had to turn around and retrace our steps—and our motorcycle ride—back to the access road and then back to the gas station, would Joe make it?

Would I?

"How about if we stop for a while?" Joe asked. "I'm getting really sleepy. Maybe we could nap until dark. We have flashlights and everything."

My watch read 3:14. "The sun's going to be out for hours, and there's no place to take cover," I answered. "We'll bake out here. We've got to keep going until we find at least some kind of shelter."

"Shelter, right." Joe stopped. He used one hand to shade his eyes as he turned in a slow circle. "There's nothing—"

His mouth dropped open. "Do you see that? Or is it a freaky desert mirage?"

I followed his gaze. We both stared at the metallic dot moving toward us. Was it—?

I yanked a small pair of binoculars out of my pack.

"It's a van," I told Joe.

7.

NOW ENTERING HEAVEN

A van. Yes! Our butts were saved.

Unless Frank and I were both having heat hallucinations. I asked Frank for his binoculars and used them to take a better look at the vehicle.

"It's a Seussmobile," I told Frank.

"What does that mean?"

"You know, it looks like something out of a Dr. Seuss book." What else was it supposed to mean?

Frank took the binoculars back and checked out the van for himself.

"See?" I asked. "It has all those weird metal things poking out all over it."

"I think they're solar panels," he said. "Which explains why we aren't hearing any motor."

It hadn't even registered with me how quiet the

van was, but my brother was right. It was as silent as a submarine under water.

"There's a good chance we've found Arthur Stench," Frank told me. "Or he's about to find us. What else would an extreme environmentalist drive?"

I took the binoculars again. The van was close enough for me to see the driver now. "It's not Stench," I announced. "Not unless he's had an extreme makeover."

A girl was operating the solar-powered van. A complete killer of a girl. With all this curly light red hair. Dark freckles on her shoulders. Shades covered her eyes—but I was thinking they were green.

Maybe this was a mirage after all.

Frank held out his hand for the binoculars. I handed them over. Then I pulled the T-shirt off my head and used my fingers to comb through my sweat-soaked hair. I'd been thinking this vacation would be girl-free. How happy was I that I was wrong?

"I'm still thinking the thing is a Stenchmobile," Frank said. "The girl could be one of his followers. There are supposed to be a bunch of people our age at the compound."

I knew that. But somehow I'd pictured Stench's followers differently. I mean, you don't usually think of normal teenager types living out in the middle of the desert. No movies. No malls. No skateboard parks. No candy. No fun.

I thought all the people at the compound would be, well, geeks. But the girl in the van was no geek. Geeks aren't hot.

Frank stared at me like I was crazy as I licked my fingers and used them to wipe the dirt off my face. "That's gross. You're smearing spit all over yourself."

Who cared? First impressions count. And the red-haired girl was about to get her first impression of me. She pulled the van to a stop next to us and leaned out the window.

"Welcome to Heaven!" she called.

"Does that mean we're dead?" Frank asked.

The girl pulled off her shades. I was wrong about her eyes. They were brown, not green. Light brown. Almost gold.

Okay, I sound like a potatohead. Sorry. Just lost it for a minute.

"You don't look like a ghost to me," the girl answered Frank. She smiled as she stared at him. Stared—as in, checked him out. After I washed my face with spit for her!

"Heaven's what we call this place," the girl added. She squinted, trying to see through the sun.

"I guess I should tell you what I'm called too. My name's Petal Northstar."

Huh? That girl's parents did *not* name her Petal. I kept my mouth shut, though. There was still a chance Petal might realize I was the Hardy who was worthy of her. I didn't want to blow it.

"I'm Alex Jefferson," Frank said. "And this is my brother, John."

Do you think he could have come up with a more boring alias for me? John. Come on. "You can call me J. J.," I quickly told Petal. "For John Jefferson."

I knew it was safer to use a fake name. But that didn't mean the name couldn't be somewhat cool.

"How'd you guys end up all the way out here?" Petal asked. Her voice was soft.

Like a petal.

Man! I just went potatohead again.

"We were just doing some off-road motorcycle riding. Then we ran over a couple of spikes, and they blew our tires out," Frank answered. "But we kept on walking."

"Maybe you should have obeyed the No Trespassing signs," Petal said. It didn't sound like she had any problem with using spikes to keep out unwanted guests.

"Yeah. It's just that you have to get almost this

deep into the desert to get the full impact of the terrain. All the way out here, the world is untouched. No soda cans. No graffiti."

Got to hand it to Frank. If Petal was from Stench's compound, he'd said the perfect words. He'd made himself look like someone who would want to live with a bunch of save-the-Earthers. I also gave him points for spitting the words out. He tended to be super-shy around girls.

Petal climbed out of the van. She walked around to the back door, opened it, and pulled out some canteens for me and Frank.

"I actually saw a cactus with graffiti carved into it once. Cut right into the cactus flesh," she said as we both took long drinks.

Nothing tastes as good as water in the desert. Nothing.

"That's so wrong," I told her. She really looked at me for the first time—then turned her attention back to Frank. I don't know how he does it. Because he doesn't even *do* anything! It's like how mosquitoes go for some people more than others. Girls swarm to Frank. And what does he do about it? Nothing. What a waste!

"Mr. Stench is expecting me back. I guess I should bring you guys with me. We can make plans to get you home later." She smiled at Frank. "Or maybe you'll want to stay awhile. Really experience the desert."

Bingo. She was definitely from Arthur Stench's compound.

"Great," Frank said. "Thanks." He climbed into the back of the van, and I was right behind him. I was hoping I could get the shotgun seat next to Petal, but it was loaded with boxes.

I wondered what was in them. Guns? Bombs? Vegetable seeds?

"Did that water taste weird to you?" Frank asked as Petal walked back around the van to the driver's side door.

"It tasted awesome," I answered.

"Don't drink too much, okay?" he said. He dropped his voice to a whisper as Petal got behind the wheel. "I think it might be poisoned. It tasted off to me."

Poisoned? But why? Did Stench somehow get advance notice that Frank and I were coming? Did he know about the mission?

The thoughts made me feel dizzy. Or maybe it was all those hours in the sun. I drank some more water. It really did taste good. Maybe a little metallic from being in the canteen, but good.

Frank shot me a disapproving look. But it's not like it was any better to die of dehydration than poison. You were dead either way.

Petal powered up the solar van, and we bounced away. It felt great to be moving *and* sitting.

"You two must be hungry." Petal said "you two" but she was using the rearview mirror to look straight at Frank. Even though Frank was still wearing a freakin' T-shirt turban and had grit all over him. He looked like one of those sand people in *Star Wars.*

"Yeah. All that walking," Frank answered.

"There are some energy bars in that bag behind your seat. Help yourself."

I didn't need to be asked twice. I grabbed bars for me and Frank, and had half of one down my gullet in about a second.

"Chewy," Frank said, the word coming out garbled because he was having trouble swallowing his bite of energy bar.

Mine wasn't going down too smooth either. The more I chewed, the bigger the lump in my mouth seemed to become. Although it couldn't really be growing.

Could it?

"Tofu and cactus fiber," Petal told us. "We make them ourselves at the compound."

Frank looked like I felt. He looked like he was about to hurl. Somehow he managed to swallow his wad of cactus tofu. I figured if he could do it, I could do it—so in one huge gulp, I forced the gunk down my throat.

"Is that what you mostly do at the compound? Cook?" I asked.

"We don't have assigned jobs like that," Petal explained. "We each do what Mr. Stench asks us to."

She answered Frank, even though I was the one who had done the asking. "She likes you," I signed to Frank, keeping my hands low so Petal couldn't see. He and I had learned American Sign Language on another mission. It came in handy when whispering was too loud.

Frank blushed. Even the tips of his ears turned fiery red. "She's pretending," he signed back. "She wants to put us off guard."

I checked to make sure that Petal's eyes were on the road and not my brother. They were. So I signed my answer. "Who cares if she is? She's smokin'."

Frank's fingers moved fast as he shot back his reply. "I don't trust her."

"You don't trust anybody," I signed back to Frank. It's true. My big brother has a suspicious nature. Which I guess is good for an ATAC member. But still.

Me? I usually trust people until I have a reason not to.

"Hey, we didn't even say thanks for saving our lives. We'd be vulture chow if you hadn't shown up," I told Petal.

I meant it. But I was trying to remind Frank that this girl had done us a huge favor.

"My pleasure," Petal said. "My complete pleasure," she added, again with the long look at Frank.

Frank's blush had started to fade—but those words from Petal got it going again.

"Hey, here we are!" Petal exclaimed. "I can't wait for you to meet Mr. Stench and everybody."

I couldn't wait to meet Stench either. The mystery man. What would he be like? Slowly, we drove past a sign that read: NOW ENTERING HEAVEN.

SUSPECT PROFILE

<u>Name:</u> Petal Northstar, aka Paula Northum

<u>Hometown:</u> La Quinta, California

<u>Physical description:</u> Age 17, 5'6", 128 lbs., red hair, brown eyes, hummingbird tattoo on left shoulder blade.

<u>Occupation:</u> Member of the Heaven compound.

<u>Background:</u> Only child; dentist father, schoolteacher mother; 3.8 GPA; created a Web page called Toxic Avengirl.

<u>Suspicious behavior:</u> Heard to say she would do absolutely anything for Arthur Stench, extremely skilled with a bow and arrow.

<u>Suspected of:</u> Aiding Arthur Stench in acts of violence.

<u>Possible motives:</u> Desire to stop the use of technology and oil.

8.

THE FAMOUS MR. STENCH

Now Entering Heaven. I wondered if that was true. Or if we were really entering some kind of hell.

Actually, the place didn't look like either. The compound didn't look like much of anything. Just a cluster of tents of different sizes, a short row of Porta-Pottis, and in the distance, one wooden building with no windows that I could see.

Petal pulled the van up next to the biggest tent. Two guys about my age trotted up to meet us. They started unloading the boxes from the front seat without a word.

"I've got some stuff to take care of," Petal said. "But I know Mr. Stench will want to see you guys and help you get wherever you need to go."

She smiled at me. Was Joe right? Did she like

me? I'm not the best girl smile evaluator.

It didn't matter. I had to stay objective. About Petal. About Stench. About the whole compound. Joe and I were on a fact-finding mission. And I needed to focus on facts. Only facts.

"That is, if he doesn't convince you to stay," Petal added. "A lot of people do. It's the kind of place you find when you're the kind of person who belongs here. I—"

"Hey, Petal. My blowin' in the wind girl," someone called, interrupting.

I turned toward the voice and saw a guy wearing a metal suit with what looked like a metal top hat on his head. Additional sheets of metal poked out from his back like mutant angel wings.

"Oh, Dorothy!" Joe said out of the side of his mouth.

I tried not to crack up. But now that Joe had pointed it out, I realized the guy did have a Tin Woodsman look going. He literally clanked as he headed over to us.

"Solar Man." Petal gave the guy a half hug. Half was all she could manage with those metal wings the guy was sporting.

"Whatcha got there?" the man asked, nodding at me and Joe.

"I found these boys wandering in the desert,"

Petal answered. "Alex and J. J., meet Solar Man. He's been with the compound from the beginning."

I made a mental note: He'd be a good source of information.

"Can you take care of them for me? I know Mr. Stench will want to talk to them."

"Of course, my little bit of flower," Solar Man told Petal.

"See you guys later," Petal told me and Joe. She headed into the large tent.

"Yeah, like she's ever actually *seen* me," Joe muttered. He's always complaining about how girls like me more. I don't get it.

"The chief is in a confab right now," Solar Man said. "Cannot be interrupted. But you two can hang with me until he's done. Come on, I'll take you to my abode."

It wasn't hard to figure out which tent belonged to Solar Man. It was the only one covered with solar panels. There was a lawn chair made entirely of foil sitting out front.

Solar Man adjusted the chair so that it was facing directly toward the sun. Then he sank down onto it with a sigh. I blinked as his solar-suit shot reflections of the sun into my eyes.

"All made of recycled materials. Found 'em myself," Solar Man told us, patting his foil chair.

"Aren't you hot?" Joe asked.

I'd wanted to ask Solar Man that myself, but I thought he might get offended.

"I'm storing up energy, little brother." Solar Man tapped a power pack strapped to his side. "Don't you think it's worth a little pain to save our planet?"

His voice was mellow, but his dark eyes were sharp.

Did he think it was worth pain to *other* people to save the planet?

"It's definitely worth some pain," Joe agreed. "I was just wondering how you can survive it. We were out in the sun for only a few hours, with no panels, and we almost didn't make it."

"I've been doing this a long time. I've built up an endurance," Solar Man explained.

I wondered what he meant by a long time. A year? Five? Twenty-five? Forty? The guy was in his sixties at least.

"Did you start when you met Mr. Stench? Or were you doing it before then?" Joe asked.

Solar Man shifted in his seat. I bet it was hard to get comfortable with those metal wings. Even if they sort of sunk down into the foil of the chair.

"I was a sun god long before I met Arthur. That's how we met, actually. He saw me gathering energy and knew I should live at the compound.

63

SUSPECT PROFILE

<u>Name:</u> Solar Man, aka Danny Sunshine, aka Daniel Templeton

<u>Hometown:</u> Woodstock, New York

<u>Physical description:</u> Age 63, 6'1'', about 160 lbs., African American, bald, brown eyes, missing one toe on right foot.

<u>Occupation:</u> Member of the Heaven compound.

<u>Background:</u> Followed the Grateful Dead selling T-shirts for twelve years; no family; no driver's license; first member of Arthur Stench's compound.

<u>Suspicious behavior:</u> Wrote a paper about how people who don't agree to use solar power should be locked in a dark cellar until they see the light.

<u>Suspected of:</u> Assisting Arthur Stench in acts of ecoterrorism.

<u>Possible motives:</u> Stench makes him feel important; Stench helps him get his message out to the world.

Even though the compound was just a dream in my man's head back then."

"How long ago was that?" I sat down in the small

patch of shade thrown by the tent. Joe flopped down next to me.

"More than a year now. First Arthur and I traveled around a little. Finding the other people who we knew belonged."

"How did you find them?"

"I feel it right here." Solar Man tapped the solar panel covering his chest. I figured he meant he felt it in his heart. Not the panel. But with a guy like Solar Man, who knew?

"I can feel their soul touching my soul. Some are like me—folks who have found their own way to make a difference." He ran his hand lightly over his metal top hat.

"A lot are like little Petal. Young ones who realize the earth is dying and have dedicated their lives to saving it."

Joe and I exchanged a look. I knew my brother was trying to make the same call I was. Harmless wacko—or should-be-behind-bars wacko?

"Arthur created a place for all of us," Solar Man went on, talking faster and faster, his voice rising with each word. "Other people—businesspeople, reporters, scientists, the president—may think we're crazy. But Arthur understands that all geniuses look a little crazy. He knows the ideas we develop here will change everything."

"I can't wait to meet him," I said.

"Be patient, tumbleweed. The man has lots of things to attend to. But he'll make time for you," Solar Man answered.

"What's that one wooden building?" Joe asked. "The one with no windows."

Excellent question. The building was definitely the winner in the one-of-these-things-is-not-like-the-other game.

"That's Arthur's thinkatorium. That's where he thinks all his big thoughts," Solar Man answered.

"And the no windows are because . . . ?" I asked, waiting for him to fill in the blank.

Solar Man sat up suddenly, solar panels clattering. "You two ask a lot of questions."

My gut muscles tightened. Had we blown our cover?

"We're curious," Joe said quickly. "Seekers."

"I like it," Solar Man told him. He turned to me. "Windows equal distractions, little brother. That's why you don't find them on Arthur's place. People equal distractions too. That's why he has a lock on the door. He needs his thinking time."

Interesting reason for having no windows and a lock on the door. It didn't seem like the most logical reason, though.

I was getting more and more curious about

Stench. No. Make that more and more *suspicious*.

"Looks like the meeting of the minds is over." Solar Man nodded to a mid-size tent. Two men walked out, followed by Petal.

"I'll take you over." Solar Man stood. "I gotta frisk you first. The chief is big on security. You have to be when you're trying to change the world. Look at what happened to JFK. And Martin Luther King."

"We're not going to assassinate anyone," Joe promised as Solar Man frisked him.

"Standard op. No exceptions," Solar Man said as he moved over to me. "Nothing personal."

When Solar Man was done checking us out, he led us over to the tent where the little meeting had just broken up. This was it.

"I've gotta go catch some more rays. Go on in," Solar Man told us. It made me feel like a little kid, but for one second I wished he was coming with us.

I pushed my way through the tent flap. My eyes went directly to a refrigerator of a man. A massive guy. Tall. Wide. With arms like slabs of meat.

"That's Mondo. He's my bodyguard. He never leaves my side."

I jerked my gaze away from Mondo and saw Arthur Stench looking at me. He was smaller than Mondo. Everyone was smaller than Mondo.

But it was absolutely clear who was in charge:

this man dressed in a long white robe, with a sword strapped to his waist. He looked like a cross between those pictures you see of Obi-Wan and samurai soldiers.

His beard was grayer than we'd seen in the photo. And although he was balding on top, he'd grown a long ponytail.

"Freak-y," Joe whispered, so quietly that only I could hear him.

Stench *was* freaky looking. Almost goofy. It was like he was wearing a costume—except that sword of his wasn't plastic. And there was something about him that made me feel like he wouldn't be afraid to use it.

"Alex and J. J. Jefferson. Can I offer you anything?" Stench asked.

Before either of us could answer, he whirled toward the wooden table to his left, whipped his sword out of the scabbard, and—*whoosh, thud*—cut one of the pineapples sitting there exactly in half.

Yeah, I was right. He'd use that sword in an instant.

Stench sheathed the sword again and gestured to Mondo. The bodyguard did the grunt work of carving the pineapple into smaller pieces. He served them to me and Joe on wooden plates.

"As you see, Mondo has many uses," Stench said.

<u>SUSPECT PROFILE</u>

<u>Name:</u> Michael "Mondo" Callihan

<u>Hometown:</u> Wakulla, Florida

<u>Physical description:</u> Age 42, 6'3", 340 lbs., blond, blue eyes.

<u>Occupation:</u> Arthur Stench's bodyguard.

<u>Background:</u> Former linebacker for the Florida Gators; two ex-wives, no kids; served a jail term for manslaughter.

<u>Suspicious behavior:</u> Bottle of steroids fell out of his pocket, observed flying into rages.

<u>Suspected of:</u> Doing Arthur Stench's dirty work.

<u>Possible motives:</u> Seems like hired muscle.

"Petal seemed to think you two might want to join our family. Is that true?" Stench asked.

"Uh, before we answer that, can I ask why you're wearing that sword?" Joe stuck a piece of pineapple in his mouth and sucked on it.

Count on my brother to ask the question everyone else wants to ask, but doesn't have the guts to.

Stench pulled the sword free again and turned it back and forth in the light pouring through the tent flaps. "It's beautiful. Elegant. Exactly what it needs to be, and no more. Unlike most creations of the modern age."

He looked at the sword like he was in love with it. "I don't allow any modern technology at the compound. That's something you need to know. I forbid it."

I would have felt better if he put the sword away. But he kept holding it out, admiring it. "We live off the land here. We live in peace with each other and the planet."

Stench sliced the sword through the air. It gave a faint whistling sound. He smiled so widely I could see the gold fillings in two of his molars.

"Still, sometimes people make their way to the compound who don't believe in peace. I need to be prepared for them. I need to be able to protect myself."

Finally Stench slid the sword back into its scabbard again. I noticed the scabbard wasn't leather. It was some kind of heavy plastic. Recycled, I assumed.

"With Mondo to protect you, who needs a sword?" Joe joked.

"Good observation," Stench said to Joe. "But

you have neglected to consider the possibility that Mondo might be my attacker."

Paranoid much? If he didn't trust his own bodyguard, who did he trust?

Stench laughed long and hard. After a few seconds Mondo joined in—but the bodyguard's laugh sounded completely fake.

"Now, is it true that you're interested in joining us here in Heaven?" Stench asked.

"We were led here, man," Joe answered. "It's like the place was calling to us. Our GPS conked out, and our cell phones went dead. Technology totally failed us. But we kept on coming. It was like we were on some kind of vision quest."

What a load of garbage. I thought maybe Joe had laid it on a little thick—but Stench was nodding in approval. I jumped in, trying to sound like as much of a fruitcake as Joe had.

"It's like that Buddhist expression. When the student is ready, the master appears." I'd heard that in some kung fu movie. It seemed appropriate. "You're supposed to be our master, man."

I could tell Stench liked that. The guy had an ego the size of Mondo.

"I wouldn't have picked you two out as part of our spirit family. A little mainstream. A little

71

clean-cut. A little too tied to the material world."

Maybe Joe shouldn't have mentioned our cell phones and GPS systems. At least he'd left his leather jacket back with the bikes. The head of the tofu-eaters would have hated it.

"That's what we were, man," Joe assured Stench. "It's not what we want to be."

"Looks can be deceiving," I added.

"Yes, they can," Stench agreed. "Do you know much about oil?"

I shrugged. "A little."

"It comes from the ground," Joe volunteered.

"Oil is the reason I created Heaven. The way we use oil is going to bring about the downfall of civilization," Stench told us. "Because soon the supply will be gone. And if there are no alternatives—which no one seems interested in developing—the modern world will come crashing to a halt."

Stench pulled his hair free of its ponytail and shook his head. "Everyone here at Heaven is expected to help stop this world-shattering crisis. It is our mission to create alternative fuel sources."

That explained why Solar Man was one of Stench's draft picks. He was all about alternative energy.

"Is that something I can expect from you?"

We had to come up with something to satisfy

him. He had to give us permission to stay at the compound.

"The wind turbines!" I burst out. "J— J. J. and I are fascinated by wind as a source of energy."

"I want to be a wind farmer!" Joe jumped in.

"Excellent." Stench nodded. "Excellent. Mondo, have Dave show the boys where to shower and bunk."

He turned back to me and Joe. "I think you two will fit in nicely. Stay as long as you like. Stay forever! There's nothing worthwhile to return to."

Mondo walked to the tent flap and whistled. Almost immediately, one of the teenage guys who'd helped unload the van appeared. Mondo gave him instructions in a low voice.

"Come with me," the guy—I assumed he was Dave—said. "Mondo said you'd want showers," he continued as we followed him out of the tent. "This is the best time of day for it. The water's been heating up since sunrise."

Forty minutes later we were showered, fed (more tofu, unfortunately), and in our own small tent.

"So besides him being freak-y, what did you think of Stench?" I asked Joe.

"I haven't decided." He rolled onto his back. "I mean, he *is* weird. But he's doing good stuff here.

73

One of the people at the compound really might come up with an alternate fuel source."

"Maybe," I agreed. "But I don't trust him."

Joe snorted. "You just don't trust anybody, Frank."

"Well—I trust him less."

9.

AN UNPLANNED MISSION

"Good morning, morning glory!" Frank said into my ear.

"Good morning, Aunt Trudy," I said without opening my eyes. "Go ahead. Dump some water over my head. It would feel outstanding."

Frank laughed. "It would, wouldn't it? But I'm drinking all I have. I guess it's not poisoned after all—since here we both are. Alive."

I sat up. "Maybe we both had a little heatstroke yesterday. Made us think twisted thoughts."

"Maybe," Frank agreed. "Let's go look around. I want to check things out without an escort."

I pulled on my jeans. The feel of the heavy material was foul. It was only about ten in the morning, but the desert was already like a barbecue pit.

That robe Stench had been wearing was probably the best thing you could wear in the heat. Not that I'd walk around in a nightgown-looking thing.

Frank led the way out of our tent. "It's like Colonial Williamsburg," I said as we walked down one of the rows of tents.

Colonial Williamsburg is this place in Virginia where we went on a vacation once. They call it a living museum, because everyone in the town acts like they're living in colonial times. No modern stuff at all.

The compound was a little like that. Not colonial, and people weren't dressed funny or anything. But there was nothing high-tech.

Which made the place pretty quiet, for starters. No TVs on. No CDs playing.

We passed a man who was using a cactus spine needle to mend a rip in a shirt, and a teenage girl who was using a frond from a palm tree to sweep the area in front of her tent.

"Isn't it kind of a waste of time to sweep dirt?" I asked her. I didn't really care about the answer. I just wanted to talk to her. She had these awesome long blond braids. And green eyes. I'm a sucker for green eyes.

"There are a lot of creepy crawlies around," the girl answered. Her eyes drifted from me to Frank

76

and stayed there. "I love them and all. And I know we share the world as equals. I just don't want them sharing my tent!"

"I'm not a creepy crawly," I began. "Does that mean I'm welcome to—"

"Hey, guys!"

The shout interrupted me. I guess it didn't matter. It's not like I was really expecting an invitation to share the girl's tent.

"How's it going?"

I turned toward the voice and spotted Dave a few tents down. He was using a hand-cranked clothes wringer to squeeze the water out of a pair of pants. The excess water fell into a bucket under the wringer.

"Hey, Dave!" Frank called. He started toward the guy.

"See you later," I told the girl with the braids. She waved at me. "Give me a call if you need help with the sweeping. We're neighbors now." I pointed to our tent.

"Both of you are staying there?" the girl asked.

Translation: I have no interest in you—but your brother is a different story.

"Yeah," I said. Then I headed after Frank. There was no point spending more time talking to Braids. She'd made her choice.

"Guess I don't have to ask how you slept," Dave said when we reached him. He dropped the pants in a basket made of woven branches. Then he pulled a T-shirt out of the tub next to him and started cranking it through his wringer.

"I think I nodded off before I even lay down," Frank answered.

"You missed breakfast, but there's probably some rutabaga muffins left." He pointed to the biggest tent. "That's the dining hall. Just go grab some if you want."

My stomach rolled over at the thought of eating a rutabaga anything. "I think I'll wait for lunch."

"Yeah," Frank agreed. "So, how long have you been living here anyway?"

Dave held up his cranking hand. "You can tell how long someone's been at the compound by the hands. I've still got blisters. That means I'm a newbie. You should see the calluses on some of the guys around here. And the girls."

He dropped the T-shirt on top of the rest of the damp clothes. "So are you two going to hang here for a while?"

"A little while, at least," Frank said.

"We're thinking we might just have found a home," I added. "Let me ask your advice. How'd you tell your parents you were moving out here?

Or did you? 'Cause I can't think of any way that our parents won't freak."

I was trying to suss out if Dave was a runaway or what.

"They told me," Dave answered. "Mr. Stench convinced my mom that this was a much better place to do her research."

"That must kind of suck for you," I said. "Being forced to leave all your friends and everything."

If Dave wasn't all that happy being here, we might get some good information from him. Unhappy people tend to blab.

"At first, yeah," Dave agreed. "But there are a lot of cool people at the compound. And I want there to be a planet to live on when I'm my parents' age, you know. And that means making some changes."

He took the bucket from under the wringer and dumped the water into the tub. "I'll take that over to the gardens later. We recycle water as much as we can."

I wondered how they got the water to begin with. I definitely hadn't seen any water sources on our way into the compound. And I'd been looking.

"So is your mom one of the people trying to develop alternate energy sources?" Frank asked.

"Yeah. You want to see?" Dave picked up the basket full of clothes.

SUSPECT PROFILE

Name: Dave Simkins

Hometown: Toledo, Ohio

Physical description: Age 16, brown eyes, brown hair, 5'11", 140 lbs., wears wire-frame glasses.

Occupation: Member of the Heaven compound.

Background: On track team before he left school; one sister in college; vegan since birth.

Suspicious behavior: Carves knives out of wood, says that humans are the worst things that have happened to the world.

Suspected of: Ecoterrorism.

Possible motives: Wants his mother's inventions to be recognized.

"Definitely," I told him.

"Come on."

Dave led us behind his tent. He dumped the basket at the feet of a short, skinny man hanging clothes on a line. "All done, Dad," Dave said. "I'm taking these guys to see Mom's lab. They're thinking of joining us."

"Welcome," Dave's dad said.

Everyone around here was so friendly. Well, except Mondo. But bodyguards aren't supposed to be friendly. I could almost see myself living here. Except for the food.

"Hey, Mom, you've got guests!" Dave called as he ushered us into the larger tent on the other side of the clothes line.

I felt like rubbing my eyes. The inside of the tent looked like the AP chem lab at school, but with even more stuff. And none of it was made with twigs or cactus needles or palm fronds.

"Mom, this is Alex and J. J.," Dave said. He turned to us. "Don't be offended if she doesn't remember your names. She's the total stereotypical absent-minded professor. She doesn't remember my name half the time."

"Not true!" Dave's mom said. But I noticed her shoes didn't match.

"What are you working on?" Frank asked. He's a science geek. I bet his fingers were itching to play with all the equipment laid out on the long tables in the tent.

"Mom just set up this system to generate water," Dave explained. He sounded really proud. "Until she showed up, everyone in the compound had to trek out to this underground spring about eight miles away and haul water back."

"It's nothing too innovative," Dave's mother said. "Everyone knows that water is made of hydrogen and oxygen, and they are both incredibly common. All it takes is some energy to combine them—solar, wind, what have you—and you get H_2O."

"And you generate enough water for the whole compound that way?" Frank asked.

"Well, we recycle whatever we can," Dave's mom said.

"But the answer is yes," Dave jumped in.

"Janet!" A plump man with Einstein-wild hair burst into the tent. He wore a T-shirt with Einstein's picture and the words GREAT SPIRITS HAVE OFTEN ENCOUNTERED VIOLENT OPPOSITION FROM WEAK MINDS on the front.

Clearly the Einstein hair wasn't an accident. I wondered if I should tell the guy that it was the brain, not the 'do, that made Einstein a genius.

"Janet, you have to come look at the machine. I think I almost have it," Einstein Wannabe said to Dave's mother.

He turned to me and Frank. "Perpetual motion," he clarified. "The secret is magnets. Who would have thought it could be so simple?"

"Everything should be made as simple as possible, but not simpler," Frank said.

Huh?

Einstein Wannabe clapped Frank on the shoulder. "Yes! Exactly! I see there is a fellow devotee in our midst."

Oh. I got it. Frank had just hauled out an Einstein quote. My brother can actually quote Einstein. I told you he was a science geek.

SUSPECT PROFILE

Name: Samuel Fisk, aka Wannabe Einstein

Hometown: San Jose, California

Physical description: Age 32, prematurely gray hair, blue eyes, 5'3", about 145 lbs., freckles.

Occupation: Member of the Heaven compound

Background: BS in physics, BS in biology, PhD in psychology; six-week voluntary stay in state mental facility; has daughter who lives with ex-wife.

Suspicious behavior: Gathers rattler venom and poisonous plants.

Suspected of: Ecoterrorism.

Possible motives: Determined to get his ideas out to the world at any cost.

"Come on!" Einstein Wannabe grabbed Dave's mom by the hand and towed her out of the tent.

Frank moved closer to one of the tables. "My mom doesn't like people in here when she's away," Dave said. "But you should come back later. She'll give you the full tour."

"That would be great," Frank said. We left Dave helping his dad hang the wash, and continued exploring the compound.

The smell of something baking took us in the direction of the dining hall tent. Whatever was cooking didn't smell like rutabagas. Or tofu. Actually, tofu doesn't really have a smell—or a taste.

It didn't take long to find the source of the smell. A rack of rolls was baking under a spiderweb of magnifying glasses.

"This is ingenious," Frank said. "Sun-powered cooking. No electricity."

"Why don't they just use a fire?" I asked.

"You mean burn trees—one of our greatest natural resources?" a familiar voice asked.

I turned and saw Petal standing behind me. "Well, yeah, I guess that's what I meant."

"It isn't as bad as burning fossil fuel," Frank said, attempting to bail me out. "No harm to the ozone layer."

"True," Petal said. "But trees moderate the climate. They improve air quality and conserve water. And animals depend on them for food and shelter."

She stepped closer to Frank and put her hand on his arm. "They are much too valuable to be used when there are so many other sources of energy."

"T-true," Frank stammered.

Yeah, he actually stammered. The guy can rappel down the side of a burning building, leap from a plane without a parachute. But he can hardly spit out a sentence around a pretty girl.

And Petal was looking especially pretty. She had her curly red hair in one of those Pebbles Flintstone ponytails on the top of her head. Is it just me, or is Pebbles hot? For a cartoon character, I mean.

"So what are the bow and arrow for?" Frank asked. He'd gotten his tongue back in working order. "Hunting tofu?"

I shouldn't rag on Frank. I hadn't even noticed that Petal had a quiver of arrows over one shoulder and a bow in the other hand. I'd been too focused on her hair.

"We don't hunt at the compound," Petal said. "You've probably noticed that we don't eat meat."

That would be a yes.

"Mr. Stench doesn't believe in eating anything

that has a face," Petal continued. "Neither do I."

"So why the bow and arrow?" I repeated Frank's question.

"Just for fun. See that bale of hay down there?" Petal didn't wait for an answer. She strung one of the arrows, then let it fly.

It hit the bale dead center.

Petal immediately got another arrow in place. I heard the string *twang*. Then I saw the second arrow neatly slice the first in half.

It was even better than Stench's attack on the pineapple. "Either of you want to try?"

A loud gong prevented me from uttering a big, "Totally."

"Time to go into town with Mr. Stench," Petal said.

Stench was leaving the compound. Score. That meant Frank and I could do some serious investigation. Maybe get into that locked "thinkatorium."

"He wants you guys to come with us." Petal propped the bow and the quiver of arrows against the tent. "Come on. He hates to be kept waiting."

Clearly, we had no choice. Frank, Petal, and I ran over to the Seussmobile and climbed in. Dave and a couple of guys we hadn't met were already in the back. Stench had the wheel. Mondo had shotgun.

I squeezed my way past a bunch of paint cans

and took a seat. I couldn't help noticing that Petal made sure to sit next to Frank.

"So what are we going to do in town?"

It seemed like everyone at the compound lived off the land, but there were a few things they had to buy. Stuff for the labs, clearly.

"Just a little mission," Stench answered for Petal. "Don't worry. You two will have fun. I promise."

A mission. I didn't like the way that sounded. You didn't call running errands a mission.

What exactly did Stench have planned?

FRANK

10.

SPLASH!

The van hit a bump. Petal knocked into me—and stayed there. Her shoulder pressed against mine.

I caught Joe rolling his eyes. It's not like I'd done anything to encourage Petal. Her name was Petal, for one thing. It was hard to imagine going out with a girl called Petal Northstar. Especially because I suspected she'd chosen the name herself.

But more important, Petal was a suspect. And you can't get emotionally involved with a suspect. That's pretty much Crime Fighting 101.

"How'd you know that stuff about how burning wood doesn't affect the ozone layer?" Petal asked me.

It wasn't a hard question. But my girl difficulty was kicking in. It's not just the blushing, which is bad enough. My tongue also seems to double in size, so I can hardly talk. And my brain goes into low gear. So even if I could talk, I wouldn't have anything human-sounding to say.

"Alex is a science geek," Joe volunteered.

Thank you, Joe. Even I could have come up with an answer that made me look less like a dork.

"I used to have a crush on Bill Nye, the Science Guy. You know, from TV?" Petal confessed. And she actually blushed. It looked okay on her. Just turning her cheeks a nice pink.

"Are you serious?" Dave asked from behind us.

"I know, I know. He's so goofy with that little bow tie and everything," Petal said. "But I just loved how he got all glowy when he talked about science. He had passion, you know?"

I inched over on the seat to put a little space between the two of us. But Petal used another bump to get right back up against me.

Joe let out an extra long, extra loud sigh. "We're almost there," Dave said, misinterpreting the cause of the sigh.

Almost there. Those words almost made me forget about Petal. The mission—whatever it turned out to be—was getting close.

I glanced up at Stench. He seemed calm and happy, but he still had his humongo sword.

The ride grew smoother as Stench pulled the van off the dirt road and onto a paved one. A few moments later we entered a small town.

We passed a park with a white gazebo in the center, then turned onto what was clearly the town's main street. Shops lined both sides. I spotted a little grocery store. A movie theater. A drugstore. Some clothes shops.

Stench pulled into an empty parking place. "Get ready," he told us. "I need to make a purchase. It's go time as soon as I get back."

He climbed out of the van. Mondo, too.

"Great, they're back," I heard someone outside say.

Dave squatted next to the closest paint can and used a Swiss Army knife to pry off the top. The paint inside was a deep red. He moved on to the next can. More red.

"So what is this mission, anyway?" Joe asked. "I'm ready for the fun!"

I knew him well enough to tell that his enthusiasm was fake. But I bet he had everyone else fooled. Joe is first-rate undercover.

"It's going to blow your mind, little brother," Solar Man said. "Just go with the flow. It makes the first time so much better."

"Cool," Joe said.

What else could he say?

"Go back where you came from, hippie freaks!" a man shouted as he walked past the van. He slammed his fist down on the windshield. Hard.

The van rocked. Paint sloshed out of one of the open cans and on to the floor. The smell filled my nostrils.

"The chief is back!" Solar Man announced.

A second later the van's front door swung open. Stench deposited a paper sack on his seat. "Let's move," he ordered.

Petal slid open the side door. She grabbed an open can of paint and stepped out. I glanced around for rollers or brushes but didn't see any.

I had an idea where this was headed. And I didn't like it.

Solar Man grabbed a can of paint, then joined Petal next to the van. Dave handed cans to Mondo and Stench, then took one for himself and jumped out.

"I opened cans for you guys too," he told Joe and me.

We picked up the cans and joined the others, huddling there between the van and the SUV parked next to it.

"Alex and J. J., just follow the others," Stench instructed. He turned his head and eyes on the sidewalk. I heard the voices and footfalls of people approaching.

"Now!" Stench shouted.

He rushed the sidewalk. Lifted the can of paint. And dumped the contents on the shoulder of a woman carrying a leather purse.

"Let the animals live!" he shrieked. "Industrial-ization is evil!"

"Killer, killer, killer!" Dave raced up to a man wearing leather loafers and doused the guy's shoes with the deep red paint.

"This is their blood!" Solar Man joined the fray. He managed to splash a woman and her little girl with one swoop of his can. Petal was right behind him, ready to pour her paint on the next innocent bystander.

I glanced at Joe. There was only one thing to do.

"Animal murderers!" I tore up to the sidewalk and splashed the paint onto the ground where there was already a puddle of red.

Joe pretended to trip. He spilled his can into the gutter.

"Back, back, back!" Stench ordered.

I joined the dash back to the van.

Two teenage boys from the town blocked our path.

The shorter one advanced. "Get those tree-loving freaks!"

11.
RUN!

A third guy joined Beefy and Scrawny—and I heard more feet pounding toward us. In a second, the group from the compound could be outnumbered.

I didn't think any of the anti-tree-loving-freak group was going to want to hear how Frank and I didn't really throw paint on anyone. Or how we barely knew the actual paint throwers.

So there was only one thing to do.

"Run!" Dave yelled.

Yeah, that was the one thing.

Mondo hustled Stench down the sidewalk to the right. Dave and Solar Man went left. Frank, Petal, and I bolted down an alley between the drugstore and Ye Olde Toy Shoppe.

An alley that happened to dead end at the back of another building.

At least there was a door. I grabbed the doorknob with both hands. Twisted. It didn't budge.

Petal shoved up beside me and pounded on the door. I shot a glance over my shoulder. We didn't have time to wait for anyone to let us in.

Scrawny and two new friends—I'll call them Red Face and Buzz Cut—were bearing down on us.

"Up!" Frank yelled.

That was the only safe direction to go. I used the doorknob as a foothold. That got me high enough that I was able to grab the rain gutter.

It creaked under my weight as I hauled myself onto the roof. "Come on, come on!" I urged Petal. I dropped to my stomach and leaned down.

Frank cupped his hands and gave Petal a boost. I grabbed her wrists and hauled her up beside me. Then Frank started climbing up the gutter drain.

The gutter held for him. Barely.

I hoped it wouldn't for Scrawny and company—because they were definitely coming after us. Red Face already had his sneaker positioned on the doorknob.

"Let's move!" Petal shouted as we got to the top of the building. She pulled herself to her feet and raced across the roof—and when she got to the edge, she didn't hesitate. She leaped across to the next one.

Frank and I were half a step behind her. And the *thud, thud, thud* I heard made it clear that the townies were right behind us.

"Get those mutants," one of them shouted.

Pain exploded in the center of my back. One of those butt breaths had thrown a rock at me!

"Over here!" Frank yelled.

He veered across the roof. "Jump!" he ordered. He hurled himself off the building.

I didn't think. I just followed my brother.

I didn't go splat on the sidewalk. I went *kabang*—on the top of the van! A second later, Petal landed half on top of me.

What's the deal? Do I look like a big foam mattress or something?

I used one hand to grab tight to one of the solar panels. I used the other to wave good-bye to Scrawny, Buzz Cut, and Red Face.

"I'm going to miss those guys," I told Frank as the van took a corner.

Frank didn't laugh. What did I tell you? No sense of humor.

The van slowed, then came to a stop.

"That was beyond belief!" Dave cried as he slid open the side door.

Frank, Petal, and I scrambled off the top of the van and climbed inside. I shoved the door shut behind us and we were off.

"Inspiring," Stench said. He sounded impressed with what the other had done.

Yeah, I thought. *Real inspiring.* We'd managed to escape from some guys who were pissed off that we'd thrown paint on a bunch of innocent people.

It's not like Scrawny and Beefy and the gang didn't have a good reason to come after us. They were the good guys in a way.

And Frank and I were in the van with the bad guys. True, we didn't throw paint on anybody. But we were there. We didn't stop it from happening. No time.

Plus, it would have blown our cover.

There was no way to feel okay about what went down. But Frank and I had made what we thought was the best call.

I glanced over at my brother. Petal was all snuggled up against him again—and he looked like he couldn't wait to get away from her.

She didn't seem quite as cool to me anymore. Not after I'd seen her throwing that paint.

Half an hour later, we were back at the compound. Just in time for lunch: spinach and tofu patties with salad.

Salad never looked so good to me.

I heaped another helping onto my wooden plate and passed the bowl to Einstein Wannabe, who was sitting next to me on the palm-frond floor mat.

"I appreciate your love of the solar panels," he told Solar Man. "But they can only take us so far. Geothermal energy is my pick. There's all that heat at the core of our planet. Just waiting to be turned into steam."

Petal nodded in approval from her seat next to Frank. "Mama Earth is ready to provide. With the right turbines you can run almost anything with steam."

"Why go to the center of the earth for something we have right over our heads?" Solar Man argued. "You don't have to dig for what Papa Sun provides."

Mama Earth and Papa Sun. Gag me with a tofu patty.

"What we need is more wind turbines," Dave's dad chimed in. He smiled at his wife. "I'm no scientist like Janet, but wind seems the way to go. There are acres and acres of land that could be wind farmed."

"The problem with that is lack of infrastructure," Janet said.

"So we set up the systems we would need to get

97

the energy to the places it's needed," Dave's father said.

"There's always hydroelectricity," a man in a long robe like Stench's suggested. "The motion of the tides can create energy."

"Why not use them all?" Petal suggested. "Sun, water, the earth's natural heat, wind. Anything but fossil fuel!"

At the words "fossil fuel" the whole group erupted. I couldn't even figure out who was saying what. "Wasteful." "Ozone destroying." "Polluting."

Stench headed over to see what the hoo-ha was about. He jumped right in. "The use of fossil fuel will bring about the destruction of civilization," he boomed.

Every head in the dining hall turned toward him. "Fossil fuel makes us slaves," he continued. "Slaves to the countries that produce the most oil. And every drop of that oil we use brings us one step closer to annihilating the earth."

Solar Man gave a hoot of agreement. Everyone else in the place applauded. I joined in. Frank did too.

"But they won't see, will they?" Stench asked. He moved past our group and began pacing around the dining hall. "We tell them and tell them, but they won't hear."

Stench threw up his arms. "We are trying to save their lives, and they call us madmen. So what are we to do?"

It felt like everyone had stopped breathing. The big tent was silent as we waited for Stench to continue.

"We give them a taste, that's what we do," Stench finally went on. "We give them a taste of the destruction to come. The only thing that will get their attention is pain."

He began to pace more quickly. "When they feel the pain, they will change. And the world will be saved!"

More applause. No one asked what kind of pain and destruction Stench was talking about. No one suggested other ways of communication.

"I have a plan. You will all have the chance to play a part when the time comes. And it is coming soon. Be ready. Stay strong. You will be given assignments when the time is right. And we will be the ones who have saved our precious planet. We will be—"

"I've gotta hit the bathroom," Frank whispered to me.

"Me too."

Guys aren't like girls. We don't go to the bathroom together. But no one in our little circle seemed to think it was strange. They were all too busy listening to Stench. Keeping low to the ground—and out of Stench's view—we snuck out.

"I figured this was the perfect time to look around a little," Frank said once we were in the clear. "Stench didn't seem like he was going to shut up for a while. And clearly he wasn't going to give any solid information about his plans."

"All that stuff about pain and destruction. I think he was talking about more than throwing some more paint."

"Yeah," Frank agreed as we walked. "The guy has lost it. I think he's capable of anything."

"Do you think he really has a plan? Or do you think it's all talk?"

"That's what we have to—"

"Quiet." I grabbed Frank's arm and pulled him into a crouch beside me. "Mondo," I whispered.

As we watched, Stench's bodyguard laced the flap of a large tent closed. Then he headed toward the row of Porta-Pottis.

"I've never seen Mondo away from Stench," I commented.

"Which makes me think whatever is in that tent is important," Frank answered. "It's too big to be his sleeping quarters. Let's check it out."

We waited until Mondo was in one of the potties

with the door shut behind him. Then we raced toward the tent. I untied the flap, and Frank and I stepped inside.

"That thing isn't solar powered," Frank said.

I couldn't say anything for a second. And that hardly ever happens to me.

"A helicopter," I finally managed to get out. "What does Stench need a helicopter for?"

"Maybe for emergencies. To get one of his people to a hospital if they needed it?" Frank suggested.

He moved up to the cockpit and opened the door. "You've got to see this."

I was still trying to take in the fact that we'd found a copter in the antitechnology compound. They didn't even use washing machines. Or have TV. And Stench had a helicopter?

"What are you waiting for?"

I hurried up to Frank and stared into the cockpit. Low airspeed indicator. Doppler NAV. Tachometer. "Notice anything weird?"

"Like what?" Frank said.

"No stick!" I burst out.

"Right. There's no way to fly this thing!"

"Can I help you boys?"

I spun around. Mondo stood in the entrance to the tent. For a huge guy, he sure was quiet.

My brain felt like a hamster on a wheel. We needed an excuse for why we were in here—but I couldn't think of anything.

Searching for a bathroom, maybe? No. A tent and a Porta-Potti don't look anything alike!

"Dave's mom invited us to take a look at her lab," Frank told Mondo.

My brother sounded completely calm. But I knew he had to be freakin' the same way I was.

"She didn't give you very good directions. Janet's lab is only a few tents away from yours."

"We were just going by size," I jumped in. "We figured the lab had to be in a big tent—and this is one of the bigger ones. Besides the dining hall. And we knew it wasn't in the dining hall."

Enough, I ordered myself. When you're lying, it's better not to blab too much. You just get yourself in trouble that way.

Mondo ran his hand over his crewcut. Did he believe us?

What would he do if he didn't?

"Go back to your own tent," he told us.

Were we under house arrest?

"We all take at least an hour's rest in the middle of the day. A siesta. It's the best way to survive the desert," Mondo continued. "You can pay a visit to Janet's lab later."

"A siesta sounds good," Frank said. We hurried past the bodyguard and went straight to our tent. We'd have to do more snooping later.

"That helicopter is definitely suspicious," I told Frank. I flopped down on my sleeping bag. "He had to get it custom-made. And why? Why a copter with no controls?"

"The only answers I can come up with are bad ones. Like you want to drop a bomb without putting a pilot in danger. Or you want to spray hazardous chemicals."

"Or spray gas and start a fire," I added. "Pain and destruction."

"We've got to work this assignment fast." Frank stretched out on his bag and tucked his hands underneath his pillow. "We don't know when Stench is going to make his next move."

He frowned and sat back up.

"What?" I asked.

"Somebody left something under my pillow."

12.

ON FIRE

"What is it?" Joe demanded.

I reached under my thin pillow and pulled out a folded sheet of paper. I opened it and read the message aloud: "Check Stench house."

Joe snatched the note away. "No signature." He flipped the paper over just to double-check. "But at least someone is on our side."

"Maybe," I answered.

Joe makes decisions quickly. I like to have more time to think.

"You think it could be a setup?"

"I think the only person I trust in this place is you," I told my brother.

"We do have to get a look in Stench's house. Possible setup or not." Joe refolded the note and handed it back to me. "The one building with a lock and no windows is definitely the place to keep information on a secret plan."

"Yep."

"You brought the lock picks, right?" Joe reached for my backpack.

"They're in there. But I have a feeling Mondo's going to be watching us," I answered. "We're going to have to choose our time carefully."

"If only Stench hadn't dragged us on that mission today," Joe complained. "With him and Mondo gone, it would have been the perfect time for a little breaking and entering."

"I've been thinking about that. I bet Stench brings every newbie on a mission as soon as possible," I said. "To make sure they're his kind of people."

"Or to *turn them into* his kind of people," Joe suggested. "I still feel slimy about today. We didn't really do anything—"

"—but it feels like we did," I finished for him.

We waited out the siesta time. If Mondo was keeping an eye on us, I wanted him to see we were following his instructions. But as soon as the hour was up, Joe and I headed back out into the compound. I did a Mondo scan. Didn't see him anywhere.

Petal, however, hurried right up. Had she been watching our tent? Had someone asked her to? Mondo? It seemed strange that she was on us the second we stepped out of the tent.

Joe here. I have to step in because Frank is so out of it. It's not weird at all that Petal came right up to us. Of course she was watching our tent. She wanted more Frank time.

Do you understand, Frank? The girl liiiikes you.

Go away, Joe. I'm telling the story.

Okay, maybe Joe's right. Maybe Petal was hanging around because she wanted to accidentally-on-purpose run into me. See my famous blush. Hear me stammer like Elmer Fudd. Whatever.

"I'm on my way to do a little more target practice." Petal waved her bow. "Want to come?"

"Sure," I said.

Joe looked at me in surprise. But I figured we needed to get a sense of Stench's routine. That way we'd know when we should make an attempt to search his house.

Why not use Petal to get some info?

"Have you ever tried archery?" Petal asked as she led the way over to the bales of hay she used as targets.

"Only a couple of times," Joe answered. "We're more track and field guys."

"That's cool." Petal stopped about thirty yards from the target. "A bullet will go about a hundred yards without any drop in trajectory. An arrow starts dropping a lot faster. That's something to keep in mind when you're aiming."

Joe raised his eyebrows. Why was this girl talking about bullets? How much did she know about firearms? And why? Just another hobby?

Petal handed me her bow. She moved close behind me and practically hugged me as she helped me position the arrow.

"Get a room," Joe joked.

Not funny. He thinks I have no sense of humor. What he doesn't get is that a lot of the time, he's not funny.

"I wish I could," Petal answered. She grinned. "I wouldn't mind giving up a tent for an actual room."

"Stench only believes in rooms for himself?" I asked.

Petal stepped away. "Go," she said. Not smiling anymore.

I let the arrow fly. It hit the hay at least.

"Mr. Stench has a lot of demands on his time," Petal told me, her voice cool. "He needs more privacy than the rest of us."

"Right. It's a thinkatorium," Joe said. He held out his hand for the bow. I gave it to him.

"Any tips?" he asked Petal.

"Aim and shoot," she told him. No hugging for Joe. He should be grateful.

"Mr. Stench really does get the best ideas in there," Petal said once Joe's arrow had landed. Landed closer to the center of the bale of hay than mine had.

"He's in there right now," Petal continued. "Sometimes, once he's inside, we don't see him for days. But when he comes out, he always has a million new plans."

For pain and destruction, I silently added.

"Days, huh?" Joe asked.

"Sometimes days. Not always," Petal said. "Your turn, Alex." She took the bow from Joe and handed it to me. Then she got her arms wrapped around me again.

"Did I mention Alex is one of my favorite names?" she asked just as I let the arrow fly. It missed the target. Entirely.

Petal laughed, but not in a mean way.

I reminded myself that she'd been hurling paint on people a few hours ago. I couldn't trust her.

I suddenly spotted Dave pushing a wheelbarrow of what looked like vegetable peelings. "Need some help?" I asked. I was ready to get away from Petal.

"Sure," Dave answered. "I'm going to add this to

the compost heap, then do some weeding in the garden."

Perfect. The garden had a clear view of Stench's house. If he came out, Joe and I would know about it.

We weeded until the sun started going down, but the door to Stench's windowless house stayed shut. Mondo left once and came back with a couple of pineapples—snack or sword practice. That's it.

When it got dark, the compound shut down. That's the way it is when you live in a place with limited electricity. (Solar Man could only do so much.)

Joe and I headed back to our tent. The sun had gotten to me again. I knew Joe was saying something, but I couldn't keep my eyes open.

I fell into a dream. I was back in the lawyer's office, where Joe and I had had our last mission. But Joe wasn't with me. Petal was.

In the dream it was easy to talk to her. And in the dream I didn't suspect her of anything.

"Do you smell smoke?" Petal asked.

I told her not to worry about it. Yeah, the building was on fire. But we could just rappel down. And it was only a dream. One of those dreams where you kind of know it's a dream.

I started to cough. Which was weird. I mean,

there was smoke in the office. But it was dream smoke. And I knew that.

Wake up, I told myself. *This is annoying.*

Don't you wish you could channel surf in dreams? But no. I was stuck in this one.

"The place is on fire!" Petal exclaimed. But her voice came out sounding like Joe's.

"Wake up, Frank!" Joe shouted. "The tent is on fire."

My eyes snapped open.

This was no dream.

Flames covered the ceiling of the tent!

13.

PAYBACK!

Frank and I grabbed our packs. As I stumbled out of the tent, a motorcycle almost ran over my toes. Beefy was on the back. "Go back where you belong, hippie!" he howled.

He splashed gas on the tent next to ours as he zoomed past. Scrawny was right behind him. Without slowing his bike down, he touched a torch to the gas-splattered canvas.

Whomp!

A fireball exploded.

A bearded man raced out of the tent and started after Beefy and Scrawny. So did Frank and I.

Helpless. We didn't have our bikes. We didn't even have a garden hose to turn on the tents!

"Bucket brigade!" Frank cried.

111

I tried to remember how much water was produced in Janet's lab. Didn't matter. We had to try something.

"There are some buckets behind the dining hall," the bearded man shouted.

The three of us raced toward the dining hall. I couldn't see much. Just flashes lit by headlights or flashlights or torches.

A Jeep zigzagged through the garden, tearing up the crops.

Red Face ran past on foot. He used a knife to slash one of the tents as he went. "This is payback!" he screamed. "You thought you got away—but we followed you. You're going down, freaks!"

A stink bomb hit Frank on the back of the neck. I didn't even see where it came from.

"Get outta here!" a man shouted as he used a baseball bat to smash the magnifying glasses of the stove.

A teenage girl behind the wheel of a beat-up convertible backed over two of the compound bicycles. She blew me a kiss as I tore by her.

And then it was over. There must have been a signal, but I missed it. The shouts stopped. The motorcycles and vehicles roared off.

The sound of my own heartbeat filled my ears as we retrieved the buckets and filled them with water.

112

But it was too late. There was nothing left of our tent to save. Nothing left of our neighbor's.

As the sun began to come up, Frank and I wandered through the compound, joining with the others in a sad, silent parade as we took in the destruction.

"Everyone to the garden!"

Stench's voice filled the compound. He spoke through the megaphone again. "Everyone to the garden immediately."

It didn't take long for everyone in the community to gather. I stared at the tire tracks running across the neat rows of vegetables. Smashed vegetables.

How long would it take to repair the damage that had been done in less than half an hour?

We all formed a circle around Stench. He dropped the megaphone. "Now, first things first. Was anyone hurt?"

There were a bunch of "no"s and headshakes.

Stench nodded. "So they stuck to property damage." He began to pace. "Can anyone tell me why you think we were attacked tonight?"

I thought it was pretty obvious. Payback, like Red Face had yelled. We'd attacked people in the town. People in the town attacked us.

Of course, I didn't say that. I was supposed to

seem like a good little Stench follower. Nobody else said anything either. I guess everybody knew Stench liked to answer his own questions.

"Oil," Stench said.

Huh?

"The oil companies have been out to get me ever since I started Heaven," Stench continued. "They know if we succeed in our mission to create alternate energy sources, they will be out of business."

Stench pulled his sword free of its scabbard. "Now, it may have looked like it was just a few hotheads from town who did this to us. But the oil companies were behind it. Oil company dollars."

Swish! Swish! The sword cut through the air.

"Yes, they're out to get us." He pointed the sword at Solar Man. "Out to get you, my brother. Because they know your way works."

"Yes!" Solar Man's panels clanked as he thrust his fist into the air.

"Out to get you"—Stench pointed his sword at Einstein Wannabe—"because they are afraid of the very idea of geothermal."

Einstein Wannabe nodded, his wild hair getting even wilder.

"They tremble at the very word hydroelectricity," Stench said to the man dressed in the long white robe identical to Stench's—the one who had been praising hydroelectricity at lunch.

Man, Stench was a genius. He was stroking egos like crazy. Making everyone feel so important.

"Those oil companies think all they have to do is pay off a few townies to take care of us." Stench brought his sword to his forehead and sighed. "They think they are so smart. With all their MBAs and scientists working for them."

Stench spun in a fast circle. "But I say that there is no one working at one of those fat cat oil companies who is smarter than any one of you."

Applause burst out in the circle.

"I say the oil companies' reign of terror is about to come to an end! We aren't going to take this from them, are we?" Stench's eyes blazed.

"NO!" everyone in the circle yelled.

I mouthed the words. I couldn't bring myself to become part of the mob. I think Frank did the same.

"Are we gonna make 'em pay?" Stench bellowed.

"Yes!" the crowd shouted back. Smiles on every face.

"You're darn right we are! Tonight at midnight is payback time!" Stench exclaimed. "Be ready. Because we are going into town!"

Cheers. Screams. Applause.

My stomach churned. Maybe this would be a good thing. I pulled Frank aside. "This is it. Our shot. They go into town. We go into Stench's house."

I glanced over at the building. It had escaped the torches.

"It is the perfect time," Frank agreed. "But we have to go into town with Stench. You heard how furious he is. If he gets too out of control, we have to be there to stop it."

"Tonight's not his big plan," I argued. "He didn't know this attack was coming. He'll probably just do something like the paint again."

"We can't know that, Joe."

"But we have to risk it. We have to find out what his big plan is. If we don't, we might not be able to put an end to it."

Frank didn't look convinced. "What if he is going to put the big plan in motion tonight? What if he decided to move up the schedule because of what happened?"

He had a point. "How about this? We know that the coptor without the controls has a part in his plan. It *has* to, right? You don't have a thing like that just sitting around."

"Agreed."

"So tonight, we hide out in the tent with the copter. We don't want to be in sight when Stench and the others leave for town, anyway," I said.

"But if Stench is putting the big plan in motion, we'll know," Frank agreed. "Because somebody will come for the helicopter."

"Right!"

We slid under the back of the helicopter tent just after sundown. We figured it was better to be hidden away early.

My biggest problem was trying not to doze off. Sitting there in the dark and everything. But that stopped being a problem when somebody grabbed me by the back of the neck.

Did I mention how quiet Mondo can be?

He looked from me to Frank. "Mr. Stench requests the honor of your presence."

14.

THE FUSE

Mondo marched us over to the van and shoved us inside. Petal, the guy Joe had named Einstein Wannabe, and Solar Man were already in place.

"You're late," Stench said from the driver's seat. "I said midnight."

I waited for Mondo to tell Stench where he'd found us. He didn't.

Did that mean the copter was a secret? Stench seemed to keep a lot of secrets from his followers.

"Lateness shows a lack of attention to detail," Stench continued as we started down the road through the desert. The solar panels had clearly stored up plenty of energy during daylight hours. We were going at least seventy.

"That can be deadly in our missions." Stench's voice filled every corner of the van.

"Sorry," Joe muttered.

"One mistake, and someone could die tonight."

"Got it," I said.

It definitely didn't sound like we were going to do more paint splattering—and that thought was confirmed by the absence of paint cans.

And something else was different from the last trip to town. Something besides Dave being replaced by Einstein Wannabe.

The van was bumping and jerking like last time. Petal had managed to get herself situated tight up against me. Mondo had shotgun again. Stench was driving.

What was it? The inside of my brain started to itch. Whatever it was was important.

I looked over at Joe. He signed one word to me. "Gas."

That was it! The inside of the van reeked of gas. And the van ran on solar power.

Something was very wrong. I scanned the vehicle, trying to figure out the source of the gas fumes. I caught Stench watching me in the rearview mirror.

"No paint tonight?" I asked. I tried to sound eager. Like I was looking forward to whatever was coming.

"Don't need it," Stench answered. His smile turned my spine to ice.

"What is our mission tonight?" Joe asked. "I'm sorry we were late—we didn't get to hear it."

Stench's smile just grew wider in reply.

"Mr. Stench gives us information on a need-to-know basis," Petal said into my ear. "He doesn't really like questions."

A leader who expected his followers to obey without asking questions. I flashed for a moment on those faces I'd seen on Mount Rushmore. Our country was founded on debate.

Did Stench know that? If he did, he obviously didn't care.

The muscles in my back and shoulders, and even my jaw, tightened as the van rolled into town. I felt Petal tense beside me. What was going to happen? *Where* was it going to happen?

We rode down the short main street, then hung a left. I took in the rows of houses. Imagining the people sleeping inside.

Was one of them Stench's target? Was he planning to use the gas to burn down one of these houses?

No. Another couple of turns and we were on a much more commercial strip. Fast-food places. A strip mall with a mini-mart. A sporting goods store. Parking lot.

Stench made a left and parked across the street from the parking lot. "Everybody out," he ordered.

I noticed he had a paper bag in his hand when he climbed out of the van. Wet splotches had appeared in the paper.

I made a point to position myself behind Stench, downwind. The gas fumes were coming from the bag.

Stench led the way across the street. A high aluminum fence circled the car lot. Stench nodded to Mondo.

Mondo pulled a pair of bolt cutters out of the back of his pants. With one snap, the lock fell off the gate. Mondo opened it for us with a bow.

Rows of bright-colored pennants flapped over our heads. A giant neon sign that read SPORT UTILITY SALE glowed in the showroom window.

They weren't kidding. The lot was filled with SUVs, SSRs, Hummers. A jeep that was probably seven feet wide. Even a monster truck that was probably more to attract people to the lot than anything else.

Solar Man let out a tortured groan behind me.

Petal shook her head. "Commercials make you think driving these things are about going off-road. Getting back to nature. But they destroy the environment."

"And no matter how often we say it, they won't hear," Stench said. "No matter how many articles we write, they won't see."

He shook his head. "Global warming, smog emissions, dependence on foreign oil . . ."

Einstein Wannabe shook his fists in the air. "No fossil fuel! No fossil fuel!"

Stench put his finger to his lips. Einstein Wannabe instantly went silent.

"We need to do more than speak and write," Stench continued. "We need to save humanity from itself. And the first thing we have to do is get their attention."

Stench pulled a damp cloth out of the paper bag. I got a strong whiff of gas. He unwrapped the cloth. I saw a coil of rope.

I knew instantly what it was for.

The rope was a fuse.

Stick one end in the gas tank. Light the other. The flame would follow the gas-soaked rope all the way to the gallons of gas. Then . . .

"Which of these gas-guzzling demons should be our victim?" Stench asked. "I say that one." He pointed to a big red SUV.

Mondo, Solar Man, and Wannabe Einstein let out a cheer. Stench started toward the vehicle.

I glanced at Joe. I could tell by his face we were in agreement. No way were we letting this happen.

"Stench!" I shouted.

He half turned, not looking pleased at the interruption.

"You think it's wrong to eat anything with a face. You want to live in peace with the entire planet," I called.

"That's right," Stench answered.

"Doesn't that include human beings?" I demanded.

"We have faces," Joe added. "We live on the Earth."

Stench jerked his thumb toward the SUV. "That is *not* a human being."

"Some human makes his living selling it," I answered. "Some human will lose thousands and thousands of dollars."

"To learn a *lesson*," Stench said. "Haven't you been listening? I do care about humanity. I'm trying to save lives."

"We're all going to die if people don't start listening to Mr. Stench!" Einstein Wannabe agreed.

"People have to see the light!" Solar Man chimed in. Stench turned back around and strode toward the SUV.

Joe nodded at me.

And we both launched ourselves at him.

I hit Stench behind the knees with one shoulder.

We both went down hard. Stench on the asphalt, me on top of Stench.

He managed to flip over on his back. He used both feet to kick me in the chest.

I flew off him, but shoved myself to my feet a second later.

Joe had managed to get one arm wrapped around Stench's throat. He was clawing at Joe's face, but Joe wasn't letting go.

I figured it was time to go for the gut. Stench's stomach was vulnerable to attack. I backed up to get a little speed going . . . and found myself dangling in the air, thanks to Mondo.

His arm was like a vise. I tried to execute a roll, but I only moved about an inch.

Mondo strode over to Joe. He snatched him up and stuck him under his other arm.

"Take them to the van," Stench ordered. "Solar Man, I give you the honor of lighting the fuse."

I felt like a sack of groceries. It was humiliating. Mondo wasn't even breathing hard when he dumped Joe and me back into the van.

He positioned himself in front of the open door.

Less than five seconds later, the others came racing back across the street. They hurled themselves inside.

We all stared out the window as the SUV exploded.

15.

NOWHERE TO HIDE

"I'm very disappointed in you two," Stench told Frank and me as he drove away. "I thought I could trust you."

I stared at the back of his head. How much did I want to get my arm wrapped around his neck again? Pretty much more than anything. But Mondo was sitting right next to him. As usual.

Want to take a guess at what was second on my list of wants?

If you guessed coming up with a foolproof escape plan, give yourself a big gold star. Because now that Frank and I had "disappointed" Stench, I thought some very *unheavenly* things were going to happen to us when we got back to Heaven.

126

So, about that foolproof escape plan. We needed one, fast. From a van zooming through the desert at about seventy miles an hour.

Hmmm.

My brain was one big blank. I looked at Frank. There didn't seem to be a lightbulb over his head either.

The ride back to the compound felt like it took minutes instead of the usual half an hour. *Think,* I ordered myself as we passed the NOW ENTERING HEAVEN sign. *Think.*

Hardly any time left.

I looked over at Frank again. He deliberately moved his gaze to the van's sliding door.

And I got it.

Between Frank and me, I was closer to the door. I pretended to tie my shoe to get a little closer.

The van slowed down as we reached the rows of tents. I made my move. I yanked open the door and hurled myself out.

Pain in my knee. In my shoulder. Sand up my nose. Down my throat.

"Get them!" Stench yelled.

A hand grabbed my arm. Pulled me to my feet. I peered into the darkness.

Frank. It was Frank.

We tore down the closest row of tents. No point in ducking into one of them. Almost every tent held a Stench follower.

And it wouldn't take the others long to search the dining hall or the lab or the tents that held other supplies. We definitely couldn't go back to the copter tent.

Racing out into the desert probably wasn't the smartest move either. It was a death trap with no food or water.

I stumbled, went down on one knee—the same one I'd landed on when I jumped out of the van. I found myself staring at a wooden shovel.

I took a moment to look around. We were in the garden.

"Frank! The compost heap!" I whispered. I dashed over to the large heap of vegetable peelings and started to dig with the shovel. Soon we heard other voices:

"They couldn't have gotten far!"

"Check all the unoccupied tents!"

"They're going to pay!"

The voices were getting closer. I dug faster. When I had a hole just big enough for Frank and me, we slid in.

FYI: slimy vegetables down the shirt—don't try it.

"There's no place to hide!" a guy called. I thought it was Dave.

"I assume they started back to town. Perhaps they found their bikes, although they would have made noise." That voice was definitely Stench's. "I'm sure they'll want to tell the police who blew up the SUV."

"Bikes. Good idea," Frank whispered.

He'd found our bikes. Shoot.

"We have to go after them. We can't let them get to the authorities," Stench demanded.

I heard the sound of footsteps moving away. "They're leaving," I said. A piece of old cabbage slid toward my mouth.

"Now what?" Frank asked. "We can't stay in here forever."

I spit the cabbage away from my mouth. "I think it's kinda homey," I answered. I thought for a moment. "We can't try to find our bikes right now. We only know one road out of here, and we could run right into Stench and the van."

"Too bad the helicopter doesn't have a stick," Frank said. "From the air, it would be no problem to find our way out of the desert."

I thought for another moment. "You know what we should do?"

"What?"

"Stench and Mondo are both away from the compound," I answered. "It's the perfect time to search Stench's house."

16.

SURPRISE!

Joe and I made a quiet trip to our tent for my lock picks. I was glad I'd decided to pack them. (I wasn't sorry about the clean underwear, either. I was pretty sure my current pair was filled with rotten rutabagas.)

Afterward we crept through the dark compound to Stench's house. Joe held a microflashlight for me while I got to work. It's not like there were any streetlights or anything.

The lock was pretty basic. I stepped inside the house and automatically felt for a light switch, even though I knew I wouldn't find—

Wait. My fingers actually felt a little plastic switch! I hit it. The room flooded with light.

"Whoa!" Joe exclaimed. He walked in and shut the door behind us. "This place is—"

"—*not* ecofriendly," I finished for him.

It wasn't just that Stench's house was wired for electricity. The lines must have been run underground. He had a refrigerator. My eyes darted around the large room. And a TV. And a computer—the latest version. High-tech.

Joe headed straight for the fridge. He pulled out a couple of bottles of water and tossed me one. "I don't know about you, but I swallowed a cup of sand. And some slimed-out cabbage."

I unscrewed the water, rinsed my mouth, then walked across the room to spit in the sink.

"Oh, man, Stench is such a fake." Joe had his head back in the fridge. "Unless they've figured out how to make a cow without a face. He has steak in here. Hamburger."

"Let's see if we can find something ATAC will be more interested in," I said. I figured the computer was the place to start.

Joe yanked the biggest desk drawer free and sat down on the floor with it. "Come to Papa," he muttered as he started shifting through the papers.

Stench hadn't bothered with a password. I guess he thought the lock on the door and Mondo were security enough.

I hit the Quicken icon. That program would let me see his banking records. How a guy gets and spends his money can be pretty interesting.

"Oh, sweet," Joe exclaimed. "That SUV Stench made Solar Man blow up? It looks like Stench *owns* it." He waved the pink slip.

"I don't get it," I said. "What was the point? What's the point of all of this? I mean, Stench obviously doesn't believe anything he says."

Joe shrugged. I turned my attention back to the computer and ran my eyes down a list of deposits and withdrawals. I hit PRINT.

"Did you find something?" Joe asked when he heard the printer cranking up.

"Oh, yeah. Stench has gotten several payments from a company called Petrol International," I told him. "Big ones."

"Petrol—as in oil? Oooh. Stench has been a bad boy." Joe raised his eyebrows as he scanned the printout. "A very bad boy. Turns out it wasn't just that SUV he owned. He owns the whole dealership."

"He's destroying the environment left and right," I said. "Hey, I just thought of something. How weird is it that this place didn't get touched when those townies came rampaging through?"

"Pretty strange," Joe agreed. "This building kind of stands out."

"I bet Stench paid them off. For some reason, he wants everyone here whipped into a frenzy."

"Ready for his plan. Whatever it is," Joe said.

I grabbed the sheet of paper from the printer. Which was right next to the landline phone.

The phone!

"Joe! Phone!" I burst out. "We can get some help."

"I can't believe I didn't think of looking for a phone first thing." Joe snatched up the receiver.

"Drop the phone, Hardy!"

17.

STENCH'S PLAN

I dropped the phone. If I didn't, I figured Stench would order Mondo to pound me into the ground.

"How do you know our real names?" Frank demanded.

Right. Stench had called me "Hardy." I'd been so shocked to see him and Mondo, it hadn't quite registered.

Stench walked over to the leather sofa on the other side of the room and sat down. "We found your motorcycles in the desert," he answered. "Traced the registrations."

He waved his hand at Mondo. Mondo stalked toward me and Frank. He reached into the kangaroo pocket of his sweatshirt and pulled out some rope.

"We know you're not an environmentalist," I told Stench.

"That rope is very low-tech," Stench shot back as Mondo began to tie my hands together. "It looks like you boys have been busy." Stench nodded toward his desk. "How brilliant am I?"

The guy's a complete loon, I thought as Mondo tied my feet together. I wouldn't have been surprised if Stench's eyes started twirling like wind turbines.

"How brilliant is this place?" Stench looked from me to Frank. "Oh. You didn't put it together."

He shook his head, making a disappointed clucking sound with his tongue. "Well, I work for an oil company."

"Petrol International," Frank said. Mondo was tying him up now.

"And what do I do for them? Well, I'll tell you. I gather up wackos." Stench brought his hand up and began counting off on his fingers. "Solar Man: my first little wacko. Samuel Fisk: my Einstein-loving wacko. Petal Northstar: my little idealistic wacko. Janet Simkins: my intellectual wacko."

Stench smiled up at the ceiling. "I'm proudest of bringing Janet here. She might really have come up with something revolutionary."

I felt like puking. "So you get paid to make sure no one develops a good alternate energy source."

"You got part of it," Stench said.

"Oh, you are so sick," Frank burst out. "I get the rest. Your job was to encourage these people to do violent things. You wanted them to look bad."

"You got it. No one wants to listen to people who are throwing paint and blowing stuff up," Stench said. "I like you two. You're smart," he added. He pulled out a cigarette and lit up. "Too bad I'm going to have to kill you."

Gulp.

I mean, I don't know what I thought Stench would do to us. But my brain hadn't gotten to murder.

"And I know exactly when I'm going to do it," Stench told us. "Tomorrow. It's Earth Day—or, at least, close enough. It was a couple of months ago. But because it's my birthday, I've chosen to celebrate Earth Day again with you."

He started tapping his toe. Then he began to sing the "Happy Birthday" song. Except half the time, he turned it into "Happy Earth Day." And he made the last line, "I'll kill the Har-dees."

Catchy.

You know what I needed right now?

Yeah. A foolproof escape plan.

I felt like Frank and I would need to be Houdinis to get out of here. We were both tied up hand and foot—and Mondo wasn't taking his eyes off of us.

"I know exactly how I'm going to do it, too," Stench continued.

I didn't really want to hear the details of my demise. But knowing what Stench had planned would make it easier to avoid whatever it was.

I hoped.

"It's going to be part of my birthday present to myself. For my birthday, I'm going to blow up a nuclear power plant."

He said it like it was nothing. Like for his birthday he was going to buy himself a pair of underpants.

"You're insane!" Frank sounded horrified.

"Oh, no. Nuclear power is *evil*. It could destroy the oil industry," Stench answered. "I've gone over the plans very carefully. The Diablo Power Plant is twelve miles from San Luis Obispo. I'm going to crash the drone into it."

The drone. Right. The helicopter with no stick.

"Great technology," Stench continued. "Very similar to what we used in Afghanistan. I can fly it anywhere from the ground. You two will be able to get an up-close look. Because you'll be inside."

He turned to Mondo. "Isn't that perfect? Even if the plant doesn't blow, these two will die. And when their bodies are found, they'll be accused of terrorism."

A blast of nausea hit me as I imagined the headlines. Imagined Mom and Aunt Trudy reading them.

At least Dad would figure out the truth.

Stench stood up. "I'm so excited. I can't wait to get started. Mondo? Would you?"

For the second time I found myself pinned under Mondo's meaty arm. He carried me outside and walked me around the building. There he dumped me into a large wooden cart that stood there. The second he stalked away I started working on the ropes. Rubbing them on the edge of the cart. The friction heated up my wrists, but I didn't feel the ropes give at all.

I stopped when I saw Mondo carrying Frank toward the cart. He tossed my brother in next to me. Then he pulled us toward the tent with the copter.

Stench trailed behind us, humming his Birthday/Earth Day song.

When we reached the tent, Mondo unlaced the flap and pulled it open wide. I could see the drone inside. The death machine.

Stench pulled a remote out of the pocket of his long white robe. He hit a button, and the drone rolled out of the tent.

"Load it up!" Stench cried. He actually clapped his hands like an excited little kid.

Mondo grabbed Frank and started toward the drone. "Petal, help!" I shouted.

She was the only one I could think of who might help us. *Might.* She liked Frank. Maybe she liked him enough to go against Stench.

"Petal!" I shouted again. "Frank needs you!"

"Like you, Petal is a little tied up right now." Stench laughed so hard that he snorted. "I made a joke!" he cried. "Your little Petal is tied up—in the desert."

Mondo came back for me and tossed me into the drone cockpit next to Frank. "What do you mean? What did you do to her?"

Stench walked up to the side of the copter. "I just did what I had to do. I found out Petal was sneaking information to you. So I had someone tie her up and leave her in the desert."

"She'll die out there!" Frank yelled.

"That's the point," Stench answered. "Everyone can't have as exciting a death as the one I've prepared for you and your brother."

He stepped back and hit a button on the remote. The propeller began to spin.

"So the note we got telling us to check out Stench's house came from Petal," Frank said. His eyebrows were pulled together.

140

"Yeah, she likes you even more than I thought," I said.

"That can't be the reason. You don't go against your beliefs because you like someone," Frank answered.

The propeller spun faster.

"Uh, can we talk about the Petal situation later?" I asked Frank. "I think we're about to have liftoff."

Not that there was anything to do. If we managed to hurl ourselves out of the copter, Mondo would just shove us back in. Maybe when we—

"Drop the remote, Stench!"

I twisted around and saw Petal with her bow and arrow. She had an arrow pointed at Stench's head.

"Get her, Mondo!" Stench ordered.

"Take one step toward me, and your boss gets an arrow through the brain," Petal told Mondo. Her voice was cold and harsh.

But it turned warm when she called out to Frank. "Don't worry. I'm gonna get you out of there, Frank!"

I assumed when she got Frank out, she'd get me out too. I mean, I'm his brother. Right?

"Dear Petal, Petal, Petal," Stench crooned. "I taught you better than that. I taught you to love all living things."

"I can love a scorpion, Stench. I can love a rattler. But I can't love you," Petal shot back.

She let the arrow fly. It hit a tree six inches away from Stench's head. "You know I'm a lot better shot than that. Take it as a warning." She strung another arrow and pointed it at the center of Stench's forehead. "Mondo, untie them."

Mondo came toward me—with a knife in his hand. Within a second all the saliva in my mouth had dried up.

Thankfully, he used the knife to cut my ropes free. Then Frank's.

We burst out of the helicopter.

"Drop the remote, Stench," Petal instructed.

"No."

Petal didn't repeat herself. She pointed the arrow downward—and shot the remote out of Stench's hand.

"Get him!" Frank shouted.

Frank got to Stench first. Tackled him. I jumped on his chest, using my weight to pin him down.

He didn't even struggle. He was staring at something over my shoulder, eyes wide. I couldn't resist taking a quick look.

The drone had risen off the ground!

"Grab it, Mondo!" Stench shouted.

I punched him in the jaw. "You aren't the one giving orders anymore," I told him.

Stench suddenly bucked, knocking me half off him. His elbow landed square on my nose, and for a second, all I could see was red dots in front of my eyes. Everything was pain.

The second my vision cleared, I managed to grab one of Stench's ears and twist. It doesn't sound like much, but it can really hurt. And it gave Frank the chance to shove Stench over and get one of his hands pinned behind his back.

"Joe, duck!"

I obeyed Frank without thinking and pressed myself flat against the ground. My hair ruffled as the drone passed above me.

"I don't know how to work this thing!" Petal exclaimed. She jabbed at the remote. "I'm trying to make it land."

Mondo lunged at her. Petal darted away, still punching the remote's buttons.

The copter jerked up, up.

Mondo made another lunge.

Then the helicopter slammed into the ground.

As it exploded, I was hit with a wave of heat. Stench twisted onto his side. "Mondo!" he cried out.

A human figure staggered out of the fireball. Mondo. He took three steps, then collapsed.

"Mondo!" Stench wailed again. And I realized he was crying. Blood and tears streaked his face.

It was over.

18.

ROAD TRIP!

Dave and his dad raced up to us. A few seconds later Einstein Wannabe appeared. His hair was wilder than ever. More people appeared every moment.

Before we could answer their questions, we had to deal with the flaming remains of the drone. We quickly formed a bucket brigade—after tying up Stench.

As the buckets of water passed down the line, I couldn't help wondering what would happen to all these people. Janet could probably get a job anywhere. But what about Solar Man?

Working together, it didn't take long to put the fire out. Then Joe, Petal, and I gave everyone in the compound as much of an explanation as we could.

Not fun.

In the background, Stench kept calling us liars. But with the blackened coptor sitting in the compound, most people believed us.

After all questions were answered, I felt it was time to wrap this case up. "I guess we should go call for—"

"Do you hear that?" Joe interrupted.

I tilted my head down and listened. Was I just having a delayed stress attack? Or was I really hearing a *real* helicopter?

I scanned the sky. Sure enough, a copter was incoming.

Ducking, Frank and I ran toward it after it had landed. Was it one of Stench's oil company bosses? Who else would be showing up in a helicopter?

The answer: our dad.

"What are you doing here?" Joe cried as Dad hopped out of the copter.

"Does that mean you're not happy to see me?" Dad asked.

"Just surprised," I told him. "How'd you find us? We barely found this place ourselves."

"That fireball helped!" Dad answered. "I was in California on a mission. I heard you two were out of cell phone range, and I thought maybe something had gone wrong. I decided to do a flyover."

Joe rolled his eyes. He hates it when Dad gets overprotective.

In this case, though, we sort of did need our butts saved. Sort of. We were just about to call for help. But somehow, calling for backup wasn't the same as being rescued by your dad. A little embarrassing.

"Do you wish I hadn't come?" Dad asked, his voice a little sharp. He'd clearly caught the eye roll.

"No," I answered. "Are you kidding? We've been eating tofu for days. We're dying to get out of here."

Joe smiled. "Yeah. We were just wrapping things up. And we needed a lift."

"And who's this?" Dad asked. He jerked his chin toward Petal. She was doing that hanging-back-but-not-going-away thing.

I waved her over. "Dad, this is Petal Northstar. This is our dad, Fenton Hardy."

"I'm Paula Northum, actually," Petal—or Paula—said.

"I knew your parents didn't name you Petal," Joe jumped in. He turned to Dad. "This girl saved our lives. Twice."

Dad shook Paula's hand. "Then I'm especially glad to meet you."

"I still don't get why you were helping us. You're part of the compound," I said.

"It's because she looooooves you, Frank," Joe butted in.

I hate to say it, but I blushed. Paula did too.

"I was in the compound undercover," Paula said. "I'm kind of an amateur detective myself. I live near here, and I wanted to find out what bigger plans Stench might have."

"And what do your parents think about this?" Dad asked. He pretty much had to. Being a parent himself.

"They're cool about it," Paula answered. "I'm home schooled, so I could be here without messing up my grades or anything. My parents and I have a lot of trust between us. They know I can take care of myself—and I've cracked some pretty intricate cases in these parts before."

She smiled at me. "At some point I started to think you were a detective too. I didn't want to blow my cover—but I wanted to help you out."

"You mean Frank and *me,*" Joe muttered. "Hi, I'm Joe. Have we met?"

"Definitely," Paula said, smirking. "You and Frank." She was still looking only at Frank, though. "Anyway, that's why I wrote you the note about Stench's house."

Paula shifted awkwardly from foot to foot. "Well, I guess you'll be leaving soon. Me too. I should go pack up my stuff."

She took a couple of steps away. Then hesitated.

"Frank," Joe whispered. "She told you she loves you. She saved your life two times. Give her your e-mail address, you moron!"

Maybe he was right, I guess. But couldn't we just go home and get to our next case?

I stepped up to Paula. My tongue had done that weird tripling in size thing, but I managed to get out a few sentences. "Uh, you want to keep in touch? That would be cool."

She gave me her e-mail. I gave her mine. You know, I probably will write. It's easier to write to girls than to talk to them—because you don't have to look at them. And they can't see you be all dorky.

"So what was *your* mission?" Joe asked our dad.

"Top secret consulting job for a high-tech security agency. You should see some of the stuff they have," Dad answered. "Motorcycles that would put yours to shame. Everything yours have, but with video cameras built right into the handlebars. Night vision headlights. Tires of a light metal alloy that can't be punctured."

"Stop," Joe begged. "I'm going to be drooling in a second."

"We have to look for our bikes," I said. "We had to ditch them in the desert, and Stench found them. Who knows what he did with them."

"I guess we might have to fly home." Joe sighed. "I'd already picked a stop on the way back. There's this mermaid show that sounded really cool."

"I forgot to mention—the security company did give me a bonus for a job well done," Dad said.

Say it, Dad. Say it, I silently pleaded.

"A couple of prototypes for the newest bikes. Gassed up and in the back of the copter," Dad told us.

Joe and I looked at each other. "Road trip!" we yelled.

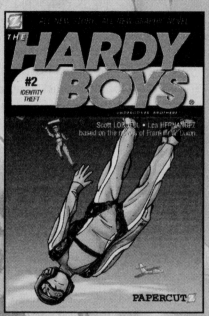

PENDRAGON

Bobby Pendragon is a seemingly normal fourteen-year-old boy. He has a family, a home, and a possible new girlfriend. But something happens to Bobby that changes his life forever.

HE IS CHOSEN TO DETERMINE THE COURSE OF HUMAN EXISTENCE.

Pulled away from the comfort of his family and suburban home, Bobby is launched into the middle of an immense, interdimensional conflict involving racial tensions, threatened ecosystems, and more. It's a journey of danger and discovery for Bobby, and his success or failure will do nothing less than determine the fate of the world. . . .

PENDRAGON
by D. J. MacHale

Book One: The Merchant of Death
Book Two: The Lost City of Faar
Book Three: The Never War
Book Four: The Reality Bug
Book Five: Black Water

Coming Soon: Book Six: The Rivers of Zadaa

From Aladdin Paperbacks • Published by Simon & Schuster